The Cave of Dreams

an Official Adventure of the

Immortal Empires™

Role-Playing Game for Mature Players

Acknowledgements

Writers & Developers

Clay Kaspers

Ben Joshua

Artists

JITT Holdings, Inc. (Cover Art)

<u>The Cave of Dreams: an Official Adventure of the Immortal Empires Role-Playing Game for Mature Players</u>

Copyright © 2019 JITT HOLDINGS, Inc.

All Rights Reserved.

62p. 8.5"x11" Full Color Softcover Laminate.

ISBN-13: 978-0-578-58158-3

BISAC: Fiction/Game/Fantasy

Table of Contents

*For these five lives
that today ye must give
I shall cause ye each
five more to live.*

-Antara Magna-

The Cave of Dreams

an *Official Adventure of the*

Immortal Empires™

Role-Playing Game for Mature Players

subrosa.games

DEAR STORYTELLER . . .

PREAMBLE...

Thank you for purchasing IMMORTAL EMPIRES™ Cave of Dreams Official Adventure! We sincerely hope you enjoy it as much as we have. Our playtesters used this Storyline every time we introduced some new players to the group...and voilà! They were hooked. Remember, this booklet is for your eyes only, and we assume that only the Storyteller is reading past this point, so if you're not going to be the Storyteller for this Adventure, STOP READING!

For this Adventure, you will need the following:
- The Storyteller's Codex
- The Adventurer's Rulebook
- 10 x White d10s
- 3 x Blue d10s
- 2 x Gold d10s
- 1 x Red d10
- 1 x Crit Multiplier d5
- 4-5 Players*
- 1 Storyteller

* You'll need 4-5 players, one to play each of the Original Element Coven members (you can play Lady Spirit if you only have 4). The Coven "Manifests" later, at which time Players will have to play two characters. Carefully observe the players during the first two Acts to see which coven personality they fit best.

Character Rank

This Adventure starts with five players who are ORank=0, freshly drawn up. By the time they "manifest" the Original Coven with the Original Elements, they should be ORank 5-7.

You'll have to plan their progression accordingly, awarding Experience and Fortune Points to get them there. It is possibly for them to survive the entire Adventure with ORank=1 characters, but this would require many CRITs in key situations.

When you get to the point of the Original Coven manifesting, you'll hand them copies of the Coven Character Records in this Adventure as they suddenly "Remember" who they are. The Coven Members are ORank=8 characters and are able to wield great power (and Coven magic with Greater Magic effect!), so make sure you are prepared! Their starting characters will be the Coven's Bonded Warriors.

Adventure Requirements

Ideally, you will have each of your players play a different Ancient Race from the other. The Original Coven is a female Arkadian (Spirit), a male Ammorian (Fire), a male Astorian (Air), a male Atlantean (Water), and a male Oshekogan (Earth). You can change it around however you wish, but this Adventure shall keep this assumption. The characters who are to become the Arkadian and Atlantean (who are thought extinct) can magically shapeshift into their "true" forms at some point later in the story.

So, your players should be Oshekogan, Astorian, or Ammorian. When they obtain the Original Elements (assuming they are successful as the quest unfolds) they will change into their true natures of Air, Earth, Fire, Water, and Spirit as the Original Coven reincarnated.

This Adventure is estimated to take around 100 hours of gaming time to complete. More, if your players are curious or you opt for the Variation of this story (see [4] on page 8).

The last requirements are that NO player's character is/has the following: Third Eye +5 (always functional), Original Magic, Greater Magic, a Marune Minion, a blood shaman, a Wyrmkyn, a dragon, an Arkadian; and, as stated before, they start as ORank=0.

Adventure Scope

This story starts out in 1135 Rome of the Astorian (northern) Empire, using the world map before The Remaking cataclysm (find a map of the Roman Empire circa 100 C.E.). You should give each of the players a short background and valid reason why they are in Rome, and bring each of them, at leisure, to the Forum at the time Scene 1 begins. It is probable their characters will not know each other at the start, but they will all hear the speech in the forum at the same time.

Hopefully, they will all be interested enough to "sign up" for the commission. If not, then you need to find a different group of players or otherwise sweeten the "hook" to get them to sign up.

After they sign up, they will start their journey from Rome towards Arkadia to gather information about the location of the entrance to the Cave of Dreams, which is somewhere in the deadly Wyrmkyn Kyngdom (the Ural mountains). You can plan encounters and personalities and maps along the way, in addition to the ones in this Adventure.

After Arkadia, they'll have to make the trek east to Wyrmkyn Kyngdom and find the entrance. Assuming they figure out how to open the portal, they enter the Cave of Dreams and the story progresses, eventually, back to Rome, but not before a couple of strolls down memory lane (back in time to the First Age) where you might have to provide some description of the world back then. You'll do good to remember that when they are back in time, certain Fighting Art powers do not work, and only Original Magic or Coven Magic works (but the characters will be able to trigger their Anchored Spells).

So, you'll have to be familiar with Rome, the Roman Empire, the lands north of Hadrian's Wall north of Londinium (Pictland, which in-game is the Arkadia they'll be going to), and the Urals. It would be nice for you to have some pictures of the areas in order to enhance their imaginations.

Preparation

[1] Be intimately familiar with this Adventure in its entirety and the rules laid out in The Storyteller's Codex and the Adventurer's Rulebook.

[2] Help the players to create their characters (we recommend doing this individually away from other players), giving guidance on Ancient Race and background. You can even role-play with them just to get them to Rome from their native countries. This will give them a richer and more believable basis for role-playing when they meet the other players' characters.

[3] Have your maps, Personalities, and your failsafe measures ready just in case a player chooses to ignore the story hook and spends too long doing his/her own thing. Failsafe measures can include meeting House Enemies, being accused of crimes, being mugged, etc. Generally, things get harder for them the further away from the story they go.

[4] You can choose to run a variation of this Adventure by having the players actually find the LIVING reincarnations of the Original Coven (instead of the dead ones as we have written herein). You'll have to come up with the extra content, but you can still hide the Original Elements in the Hidden Vale. The game accessory, *Atilius's Journal,* chronicles this variation from former Cloud Dancer Bernardin Atilius Lupus's point of view.

Personalities You'll Need

Below is a list of Personalities you'll need for this Adventure whose stats are not in this Adventure but in the Storyteller's Codex:

Major Personalities
- Vestal Virgin Aunt Julia
- Empress Maximina Julia
- Optimus Annius Verus
- Maximillian Rufus
- Ophelia Hadriana
- Queen Brûd
- Simcha
- Anyone else you want for a side-story

Minor Personalities (Optional)
- Adolfo Maximus Mactator (Maximillian's Primus Pilus)
- Bernardin Atilius Lupus (Cloud Dancer Assassin)
- Optima Hadriana (Ophelia's sister)
- Octavian Hadrian (Ophelia's father)
- Albanaeus Rufus* (Maximillian and Optimus's cousin)

* More information on Albanaeus is provided herein, as he is not mentioned per se in the Minor Personalities section. But you can see his attitude from his notes on page 123 of the Storyteller's Codex (as well as get a feel for him from the Immortal Empires of the Seventh Age novels).

You can add other Personalities as you see fit.

World Setting at Start of Play

The Astorian Empire is at peace, finally having vanquished all of its enemies and conspirators under Emperor Scipio through his great general Maximillian Rufus. To celebrate the young warrior's accomplishments in slaying two of Emperor Scipio's arch enemies in just seven days, the Emperor had just days ago pro-moted Maximillian to the rank of Legate of the Tenth Legion and given him the exalted title "Praedatorus." It is public knowledge that Maximillian Praedatorus killed the usurper Stilicho and then later the Southern (Ammorian) Emperor Gratian using his Arvalis skill with a two-handed Astorian Great Sword. He is therefore a symbol of national pride among the plebs and greatly celebrated by them, and held in even higher esteem by the Arvals.

Emperor Scipio has awarded Legate Maximillian with a Tri-umph on the day the story opens. It is a great spectacle, with the whole Tenth Legion driving before them slaves of the conquered, riches of cities that fell, and captured relics, all to be gifted to the Emperor. Having heard of Maximillian's renown, foreigners from far and wide have lined the city's streets hoping to get a glimpse of his glory.

As for other lands, the Ammorian (Southern) Empire is de-feated, for now, having been deceived by a Magnus Maximus, a Marune Minion, who was defeated by Maximillian. Their Mag-isterium of the Antaran philosophy is busying themselves with looking for a suitable imperial replacement for the slain Gratian, in addition to making it illegal for any Ammorian citizen to em-igrate to the Northern Empire (no one likes to be on the losing team).

The Arkadians are still in hiding as all their Fey are still locked up in the Cave of Dreams. Hadrian's Wall was built to keep the ferocious Picts, who are companions to deadly magical animals, out of the Astorian Empire. These deadly "magical animals" are really shapeshifted Arkadians. They allow all to think that they disappeared with the Fey into the Cave of Dreams.

Atlantis, likewise, is nowhere to be found (at least to anyone who isn't Atlantean). It is hidden deep in the "Greater World" (the ocean), and purported to be destroyed in the Second Cat-aclysm, which was during the Age of War. Atlanteans walking around on the Lesser World (land) are very rare, still, and avoid-ed by most as a mystery.

Oshekoga ignores the rest of the world for its own, never-end-ing feuds between Warlords, none of whom can seem to become powerful enough to unite the vast Oshekogan lands into one em-pire. Most Oshekogans, then, who venture away from Oshekoga are seen as either great warriors on leave or those who have fled their masters and become despicable deserters (ronin).

The Ancient Races rule the world, which, with the exception of Oshekoga, is at peace. The Starborn and Newborn know well enough to keep quiet and in line, lest they incur the wrath of a powerful Ancient Race and their magic. The Cave of Dreams is still closed and is now only a topic Master Scholars discuss (to the rest, it has been forgotten, although it might appear in some families' bedtime stories). Original Magic does not exist (having not been around since the Age of War). Dreamwalking is an art known only to a very few, having been lost to the world when the Arkadians disappeared. The dragons are not in the world either, having disappeared with the Fey in the First Age.

ACT 1: TRIUMPH

Here we go. For the remainder of this Adventure, regular text is for your eyes only. We will put text that you may want to read to the players in italics. Special Instructions and helps will be in blue italics.

Should you want to play the videos that accompany the description, you'll need an internet connection (you may have to endure ads, unfortunately!). We try to do an educational video for you and an action video for your players' edification. Please notify us if the links do not work (as links sometimes change) and we will do our best to find a similar video to link to. Links are provided for educational purposes only.

Assuming You've Gotten each player safely to Rome during the day of Maximillian's Triumph, you're ready to begin the Adventure in earnest. Enjoy!

ST VideoLink: *http://immortalempires.com/triumphst.mp4*
PL VideoLink: *http://immortalempires.com/triumph.mp4*

ROME

The Astorian Emperor has spared no expense in this triumph! Instead, it is obvious he is using Maximillian's victories as a symbol of Rome's might and wealth, a grand reminder of its preeminence among all nations. While the Emperor himself had not yet appeared (and has evaded all eyes ever since the war ended), his vassals were everywhere preparing the day.

Master Scholars in rainbow-trimmed robes and iron-clad Praetorian Guard captains commanded their inferiors. They used magic to banish all clouds and rain. They used soldiers and swords to push the excited crowds to the sides of the streets. Everyone everywhere was talking or shouting. There were so many foreigners that the guards had simply ceased to ask them for their papers, entrusting the job of city security to the myriad Arval Brothers and Arval Sisters who scanned them with black eyes to make sure they were not assassins.

Powerful Vestal Virgins in white dresses floated high above the city, strictly enforcing the 'no flying' edict the Imperial Household

handed down for today's triumph.

Opulence everywhere gleamed on the city's Olympus-sized colonnades and temples, as well as every citizen's best clothing. Gold and jewels of every color hung on people or high on city walls below patrolling guards.

In the distance, trumpets! The triumph was beginning. Soon, history's youngest Legate Maximillian Rufus Praedatorus, at only twenty-two years of age, was going to pass by having started his Triumph outside the city in the Field of Mars. Usually, the triumph would lead through the Forum Romanum and Circus Maximus and end on the Capitoline Hill. But today, the Forum was to be last. Evidently, the Emperor himself was going to give an important speech there.

Hopeful children who dreamed of entering the Legion and pursue the Cursus Militim stood by anxiously awaiting just a glance of recognition from Legate Maximillian. Perhaps some of them would be so brave as to go before his four-horse-drawn chariot (a Quadriga) and throw a rose up to him. If he caught it, it would mean their dreams would come true! Someday, they would be a great general like him.

At this point, you should ask the players where they are (and have a map of the city with the proposed Triumph path handy for them) and what they're doing. Are they going to anchor a spell? Perhaps position themselves to also get attention from Maximillian? Attempt to talk to a guard or a Scholar making preparations? Do they have to go buy a rose to throw at Maximillian?

Although the crowd adds to what seems like mayhem, the people are genuinely excited and happy. Any criminal acts will be reported immediately, or challenged directly by bystanders hoping to draw the attention of the City Guards, the Praetorian Guards (who are much more deadly), the Vestal Virgins, or the merciless Arval Brothers/Sisters, who have the power to execute lawbreakers in a summary judgment, having only to answer to the Emperor himself.

Mark down any secret Target Numbers they've done that you may need for later. Tell them the results of any Magic or Synergy Talents they used.

Hopefully, the players are making their way either to Maximillian or to the Forum, where Maximillian will give honor to the Emperor, handing over the dead bodies of Gratian and Stilicho, many captives, and treasure (gold, relics, etc.) in Tribute (because everyone wants to see that, right?).

If needed, embellish with your own details the Triumph activities and description of the parade, until such a time as Maximillian finally arrives in the Forum Romanum.

FORUM ROMANUM

Today in the forum there is no vendor, no haggling over price, no dozens of speeches given by various philosophical advocates. There is only the people of Rome shouting for joy for the pride of winning the year-long war against the Southern Empire. Any moment now, and the Emperor will appear in all his glory, the true Avatar of Astor, with the piercing Sun beaming from behind the clouds in his Skyborn Eyes. He will give a speech, and then bless the people. Everyone seeking this Avatar-level blessing is pushing to be in the forum. Some fights have broken out, since there is barely standing room, and the people who have followed Maximillian all the way here can't seem to get within the forum's boundaries. Guards are swift to arrest those caught fighting. As soon as they place manacles on them, the lawbreakers disappear to some unknown dungeon far beneath the city, so it is rumored.

The players' characters (henceforth: players) need to find a way into the forum without causing a disturbance, if they want the Emperor's blessing. Once they're in, they'll want to get in further to avoid the fights breaking out on the fringes. If they don't, they might have a violent encounter which they would be wise to run away from before they are caught by the guards (and sent to the underground dungeons of Tullianum, a temporary holding prison on the northeastern slope of the Capitoline Hill).

Once the players situate themselves, continue.

The raucous cheers of the people die down slowly as Maximillian steps off the chariot towards the dais where stand the Emperor's sister, Maximina, and the rest of the Imperial Household. He brings the one rose he kept as a gift for Maximina, who graciously accepts it and then hands it to the leader of all the Vestal Virgins, Aunt Julia, who looks remarkably young for her advanced age. You know this and that Aunt Julia is a powerful immortal from all the whispers around you of parents telling their children the same.

If any of the players threw a rose up to Maximillian, you should have rolled to see if he caught it and kept it. He would not have kept it until his chariot turned into the forum. Other roses that he caught, he would have kissed and thrown back to the person who tossed it up to him. Such a rose would have a minor blessing on it that lasts days. If the player's rose is the one that is gifted to Maximina, they will have a pleasant surprise coming later. For now, make sure you describe how Maximina graciously accepts the rose and then gives it to Aunt Julia, the Vestal Virgin, standing next to her.

There is still no sign of the Emperor, though. Anyone casting an ear can hear multiple whispers of what this might mean. Is the Emperor refusing Maximillian's glory, after all? Has he fallen ill?

Maximina, dressed in a pure white toga with purple trim, a wreath of purple carnations in her ornately braided and woven blonde hair (in true Roman style on top of her head), steps forward from her retinue to greet Maximillian. Her voice, amplified by magic, easily carries throughout the spacious forum and quiets the whispering hiss of conjecture.

"Conscript Fathers, Senators, Patricians, Equestrians, and our beloved Plebeians, we are here to celebrate Maximillian Rufus Praedatorus, our greatest general since Hadrian. My brother, the Emperor..." Maximina paused, as if changing her mind about what

she was going to say.

"...had to leave suddenly on important business and regrets not being here for this great celebration of Rome's great victory." Whispers hissed across the forum again. Ignoring them, she continued.

"This day marks the last day of our week-long celebration of Rome's victory over our enemies. Now, all of Astoria is at peace, and our preeminence cannot be questioned. But enough of my blabber. It is time to give honor to all of you, the people and friends of Rome! Lower your resistances and I shall give you my blessing."

At this time, ask each of the players if they lower their resistances to receive Maximina's blessing. But interject the following scene before you reach the last player's decision:

Suddenly, a old man screams "NO! Don't." and forces his way past the guards around the dais. He is dressed as a Master Scholar with a rainbow trimmed toga and gleaming white stone ring he magically received from the Great Plinth at Rhodes when he graduated the Academy. The crowd's whispers act up again. But he bellows out all the more: "The Empress, the Empress is a Marune! Don't listen to her! She has the rainbow eyes of a Marune!"

This is, of course, Master Scholar Albanaeus Rufus, Maximillian's cousin, but the players wouldn't know that unless they make an Awareness TN:20 to hear it among the shouting and frenzied whispers. Some are saying he's just jealous Maximillian is receiving honors. Others say he's always been a little crazy.

The guards finally get a hold on the old Master Scholar and drag him away, towards the Capitoline Hill's prison, no doubt. The guards do not bother silencing him, apparently preferring instead to let the old guy embarrass himself: "The Empress is a Marune! The Empress is a Marune!" His shout diminishes the further he is dragged away, and yes, he is dragged towards Capitoline Hill.

When his shouts are barely audible, Maximina starts again, laughing somewhat, and bringing Maximillian on the stage with her to face the crowd.

"Well, I wonder who he is talking about. Last I checked, I was not an Empress, only the sister to the Emperor." Her statement was met with several giggles in the crowd. "Poor Albanaeus," she continued, "perhaps all his learning has proven too much for him. I will ask the Vestals to look after him. But now, my beloved fellow citizens and you friends of Rome who with us celebrate our victory, prepare yourselves to receive this Greater Blessing."

Now ask the last player if he's going to lower his/her Magic Resistance to receive the blessing, and then see if any other player wants to change their previous answer.

Now secretly roll Maximina's Potency: 10d10g (Since it is Greater Magic, any Potency that gets through the lowered resistance is multiplied by 5 to serve as the Binding of the Blessing. In this one case, Maximina has chosen to not force this Blessing upon anyone who hasn't lowered their resistance.) Subtract rolled lowered MResists from the Potency you rolled and multiply that by 5. Write this down for each player on your own Adventure notes (the players should not be privileged to know what the Binding is; they would have to perform a Magical Diagnosis to know that).

For anyone who received the Blessing, you can tell them in so many words this (You can formulate a blessing speech that Maximina will say that incorporates the following):

- +[M] die to SK:Seduction, SK:Casting, SK:Appraising
- +[M] die to SK:Law, SK:Aura Reading, SK:Hunting
- +[M] die to SK:Horticulture, SK:Dancing, SK:Cooking
- +10% Attraction, +6/Day Heal Rate
- Lasts 1d5 Weeks

But DO NOT tell them that secretly interwoven with the Blessing is an IMPLANTED CHARM that does the following:

- Oblivious Charm: Verbal Suggestion: Shouldn't [10]: "Support Maximina to be your next Empress!"
- Oblivious Charm: Engender Overbearing Affection for Person: Maximina (You can explain this by simply stating she looks beautiful to them, as if it could be explained away by the Attraction boost they also received.)
- Oblivious Charm: Verbal Suggestion: Against Nature [50]: "Defend Maximina to the Death"

Remember that the number in brackets after the Charm level [10] or [50] means the Differential TN (DTN) that Maximina's Potency must be above the rolled MResist of those who accepted the blessing. If that DTN was not reached, then that particular Charm does not have any effect on that person. For purposes of the Crowd, assume 60% of the crowd fell victim to all the charms, and will defend Maximina to the death if anyone speaks ill of her; assume 90% of the crowd will support Maximina to be their next Empress.

If a player fell victim to one of the implanted oblivious charms, you'll have to notify them secretly on how they should role-play their character, without telling them they have a charm! If they role-play well, reward them with extra FPs and Experience.

GATHERING "VOLUNTEERS"

It's possible that a couple of the players could have met each other (in character) during the Triumph. If one of the players was hauled away to prison, they'll have to become "volunteers" for this next task to earn their pardon from the Emperor.

Assuming none of them are imprisoned, it will be your job to create mystery enough to get them seeking out the truth behind why the Emperor really didn't appear at the Triumph.

In fact, the Arvals are talking with one another when they think no one can hear them, after the celebrations are over. The Arvals will be monitoring the last night of the raucous celebrations, sneaking a drink here and there for themselves while on duty. So, they will be in the bars and taverns and on the street, in groups of two, three, or four.

Some fights will break out between those who were completely charmed and those who might think the Empress killed her

brother just to become Empress, and that maybe Albanaeus was right, that she is a Marune, or at least a Marune Minion.

In all of these scenarios, the players might overhear the Arvals talking thusly (use can use SK:Info Gathering, SK:Interrogation (if they take a chance at directly confronting an Arval - dangerous that!), SK:Mingling, or SK:Lip Reading at trying to hear these conversations. They can also use magic: Utility School:Audio Eavesdropping (they will not need Potency since the Arvals will not be talking in a Sound Bubble; they'll just need to successfully cast the spell; note that a successful spell bypasses all TN requirements below). Target Numbers for these skills precede the tidbits. Each TN represents a different speaker who may be in a completely different place than the other speaker (depending on where your players are).

[TN5] *Do you feel weird after that Blessing? I'm very thirsty all of a sudden, like I can't get enough wine! Hahaha! Come, let's drink to Maximillian!*

[TN10] *Maxima should have just told the people the truth. She started to, but then changed her mind. Did you see that?*

[TN10] *Well, Albanaeus is Optimus's cousin too, and I hear he's paying gold auraes for someone to smuggle Albanaeus out of Rome.*

[TN10] *The Emperor's never been sick a day in his life. He's obviously sick of Maximillian's self-aggrandizement.*

[TN10] *Well, if Maxima were a Marune, don't you think that the Vestal Virgins would know? I mean Aunt Julia was standing right next to her!*

[TN10] *No one cares about what you think Brutus. You'll do as your told and not mention anything to anyone about the Emperor's disappearance. Slip up and I'll crucify you myself.*

[TN15] *Well, while he's missing, Maxima is obviously going to step in as Empress. No doubt, that's really what's going on. It's about time we had a woman giving orders from the top.*

[TN15] *I heard he went to save his friend Mulchus from a band of Wyrmkyn shapeshifters. Emperor Scipio wouldn't have missed the Triumph of his own volition. Hell, Maximillian nearly single-handedly won the war for him. It would be politically dangerous for Scipio to snub him.*

[TN15] *The guy is senile! You can't change into a Marune. Yeah, a Marune Minion maybe, but not a Marune. He's obviously walking with one sandal-strap loose.*

[TN20] *I'll have to ask Optimus if I can volunteer. Imagine being the one to come back with him. I'd have a triumph of my own!*

[TN20] *I wouldn't want to do it. No one's come back alive from beyond The Wall...ever. No wonder they're looking for volunteers.*

[TN20] *Well, Ophelia did say that the Sibylline books said something about the return of the Faeries, eventually. But the Lying Oracle of Sydyll also is known to utter that if they open one door, another will close. So, I say, leave it alone. Why monkey with the unknown and fuck up the present?*

[TN30] *Oh, you're just a coward. I volunteered and received a hefty advance, see? [shakes a large purse of coin] Come on, Silvanus, let's go see Optimus. He knows we're friends and we work well together. It'll be like the old days in Liguria. What do you say?*

[TN30] *[a foreigner obviously not Roman] Yeah, they paid me up front. Promised me more and Roman Citizenship if I made it back from Pictland with some information about their emperor. Seems like he told someone he was going there to seek the Arkadians, who, everyone knows, have been extinct since the Cast of Woes.*

[TN40] *[Maximillian Rufus and Ophelia Hadriana talking] Stop being a cheapskate, Max. You need to dip into your family's wealth and scrounge up some pay for our volunteers. Magic Travel is not allowed beyond The Wall, you dolt! Not even if you wear a hat the size or your ego! Even a First Degree Scholar knows that.*

Well I'm no scholar, Ophie, but I know a fool's errand when I see one. If Scipio wanted people to know where he was, he would've told us. He's an Avatar, for Astor's sake! And you think he was kidnapped by extinct Arkadians?

[TN50] *[Optimus talking with a raid party] So, after you receive some magical protections, money, and a couple of magically enhanced weapons and such, you'll simply swear an oath to carry out this search and then give the Green Man this small scroll to give to the Arkadians. Ignore everything you think you know about the world, that Arkadians and the Cave of Dreams are just myths, that Wyrmkyn and Blood Shamans only come out at night. You're about to find out that it's all real. And, that it's all very, very dangerous. Still want to go? I understand if any of you want to drop out now. I'll simply cast a Greater forget spell on you and let you go back to your no account lives so you can go get laid and drink your liver into oblivion. Oh, and I might just strip you of your citizenship too, for being such cowards! Now, who's ready to swear the oath?*

[TN100 or CRIT] *[Empress Maximina talking with Aunt Julia] If you are a Marune Minion, Maximina, I'll eventually find out and tear you limb from limb...with your own hands.*

Yes, well, if I were you would have known that already, right? Or did you lose your power to penetrate everyone's mind? The fact is that my brother is trapped in the Cave of Dreams. We don't know why he went there. We don't know how. But we do know that he sits a Red Crystal Throne in that Power-forsaken hell. And only the Arkadian DreamCarvers know how to get into the place. So, while I appreciate your concern for my own well being in that I remain free from corruption, I'd very much more appreciate it if you started focusing on how we can "wake" the Arkadians without appearing like we're invading their land and starting another all out war on the heels of our victory.

You can make up more rumors and red herrings, but you need to prepare to role-play each of them. For instance, the smuggle Albanaeus out of prison scenario is a red herring, and if they do that, they'll be rounded up and put in the prison (maybe that's where all of the players will meet each other...).

Odds are that your players' ORank=0 characters will not be able to reach the higher TNs to find out what's really going on, so your job of getting them introduced to each other might be that much harder. Remember also, that just because they are of different races does not mean that they are not Roman citizens. So, they might feel loyalty to the cause even without your prodding.

Assuming you've finally got your players' characters acquainted with each other and willing to work together, they'll have their audience with Optimus, Maximillian, and/or Ophelia (however you want to do it).

An oath is administered whereby the characters agree to seek out the Lahavian Green Man or any Arkadian north of Hadrian's Wall and deliver the small scroll to them. The small scroll is sealed with Maxima's Seal, but only for protection. It reads:

DreamCarver, I implore you by the Youth of the Maiden, come to my aid and give me knowledge on how to enter the Cave of Dreams. My brother is trapped therein. Please help and you will have my song for as long as I live.

Most Respectfully, Maximina Julia Astorica

This scroll is written in Ancient Astorian and Ancient Arkadian. Each member of the party is also given one of each:

1. a belt purse of 100 gold aurae

2. one MenH-L weapon of B=25L which gives +[M] to their Skill they use to attack with (Weapon Category) and +1T1 to damage for that weapon

3. one MenH-L armor piece of Total Body DV=10, B=25L (10 DV to each arm, each leg, and to Vitals)

4. one MenH-g Ring that is a Spell Repository for a Message Spell to [Optimus, Maximillian, or Ophelia] of up to 10 words and also serves as a Divination and Travel Link, as well as a Secondary Focus for Curative and Defensive Schools B=5g

They are fed, given adventuring clothes (and heavy sagums to keep them warm against the cold upper reaches where they'll be heading). They're allowed no more than twelve hours to get their affairs in order, but then must promptly report back to [Optimus, Maximillian, or Ophelia] in order to receive whatever active spell protections you want to give them.

After that, they are Traveled to just south of Hadrian's Wall (north of Londinium), where they will meet the very strange, very eccentric Lahavians.

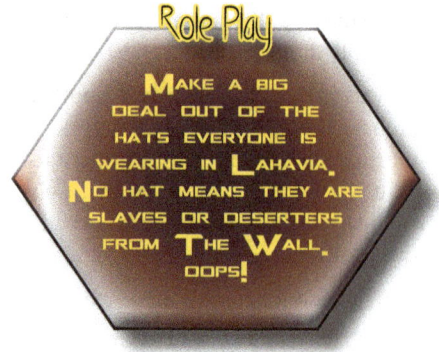

ACT 2: THE JOURNEY

LAHAVIA

They might seem small-minded at first, with their simple names for things "Wall street (for the street along The Graywall), Center Tower (for the center tower), Stone House (for the only house south of the Graywall that is built of stone...but the Lahavians are devious gossips always trying to outdo each other on the social scene.

They regard foreigners with contempt, deeming even the Ancient Races as "slow" and "inept" in that they always appear confused at the *more civilized* Lahavian way of life, which involves hat pissing contests (even between women) to see whose hat is bigger and more ornate, fights to the death for Dukedoms, and all manner of so-called eclectic discussion which aims (always) to belittle and smear the opposing side of the argument.

Lahavians are not afraid to scrap with the best of them and many a presumed victor has been sent away to The Wall for murder (its proper name is The Graywall, but common vernacular sounds more threatening: "I'll send your ass to THE WALL, you BASTARD!"). To avoid being sentenced to The Wall (which is usually a life sentence), those fighting must find a way to end the fight before someone dies while allowing each fighter to keep face.

Sometimes, all that is needed is for the soon-to-be-dead losing combatant to suddenly compliment his stronger opponent's hat, or, if he has a better hat (which could have been the cause of the fight in the first place as being too glorious for his lowly station) to offer to trade. Such a gesture is respected and there is no association of cowardice with it.

These tidbits (and those from the core game books) about Lahavia can/should be researched and discovered by your players during their allotted 12 hours before they are Traveled here. If they don't, getting past the Graywall into Pictland might take a little longer than they hoped...

In the Appendix, you'll find spells and stats for various Personalities we've introduced here. Feel free to modify them to suit your own tastes and players if you feel ours are too low or too over-powered (for instance, if you want to embroil the players in fugitive status by allowing them to kill the arrogant First Horse, you might make First Horse weaker...then they would have to flee quickly from The Graywall into the unknown Pictland which leads to the dangerous and magical Arkadia.

MIDTOWN

A little unnerving for those not used to it, to be sure, Travel magic placed you instantaneously in different surroundings in the blink of an eye. Instead of the smell of Rome's bakeries and smoking meats, you smell the stench of manure and pasture. Indeed, you're standing at the northern edge of a grassy field where cows are grazing. They don't seem to mind your being there.

A mile or two to the north, you see Hadrian's Wall spanning

the horizon as far as you can see east and west. It's larger and taller than you thought, and it looks like the Graymen, condemned prisoners, all, are patrolling on top of it and walking all around the small village you're standing just south of.

Directly in front of you is a signpost that reads: "Midtown. Population: 2000 1994 1900 2010 1600 1845" and so on as it is covered on both sides with numerous updates. A young man, boy, really, of about fifteen years, is heading toward you with another signpost, this one with only one number on it. He is dressed in drab gray with a heavy fur sagum that looks like it has been darned in at least a dozen spots. He wears a small gray hat that is pulled down over his ears.

Ask for actions of players.

The boy is Morgan Elliot, and he was born a Grayman (ORank=0). His mother was sentenced to The Wall twenty years ago for not cleaning a Duchess's tub very well. She still lives with him in Midtown. He knows all about Midtown and Midtower, who First Horse is, what dangers lurk beyond the Wall, but he's not old enough to go (that will happen when he's 16). Of course, the players are free to ignore Morgan or whatever, but they'll miss getting the scoop on the mean old man called First Horse.

Morgan is simply replacing the old signpost with a new one that has more space to write more population updates as new prisoners arrive and old ones die.

Storyteller: take it from here...Perhaps you can give the players another go at learning some of the gossip they may have missed in Rome if they wander around Midtown's taverns. People here would not be interested, really, but you could place a Bard personality here just to gossip about what was going on in Rome. S/He'd be delighted to share what s/he knows for some heavy Roman coin from the players!

MIDTOWER

Rising at least another 30 large Astorian feet from the 20-foot high Graywall is Midtower, the administrative building that governs Midtown and the Graymen assigned to this section of wall. While it looks like a fortress from the outside, there are no guards checking the gray-clad soldiers as they enter. Everyone looks completely free to enter and leave the tower.

The Graymen don't really speak to Outsiders, especially those who are not Lahavian. First, they know only a Duke has the power to free them. Second, they know that foreigners at The Wall can only mean one thing: trouble.

Inside Midtower, there is just one personality of note: Bandy Gall, Governor of The Graywall, who is technically First Horse's boss but cowers in his presence. First Horse will be out conducting a sweep north of the Graywall when the party makes its way in. Bandy Gall is technically a Duke (Duke of Graywall) but is himself banished here as a punishment, and cannot take the title nor wear a Duke-worthy hat.

BANDY GALL: GREEDY, SARCASTIC, CAUTIOUS, SPITEFUL					
PHQ	3	TAC	0	MResist: 2d10g +	1
PHL	1	SOC	1	PResist: 2d10g +	2
AGL	1	CBT	0	Awareness:	5
COR	0	END	0	MTAP:	40
INT	1	ART	0	SK:Crushing Weapons	R4
INS	2	MYS	0	SK:Bows	R2
WIL	3	BV	160	SK:Dodge	R1
EMP	1	DV	5	Other Primary Skills:	R1
MAF	0	MVT	3	Synergy	49
ORank=1 (Politician/Starborn Lahavian): +4 LUCK (one roll per day), Talents: Disparaging Rant Diatribe (AR124), COR5:One Foot Fighting; Favor Bank: 2 Small Favors that he can do, 1 Small domestic Favor he can ask. Bandy has a wooden leg (left, knee-down), that falls off from time to time, especially if he moves quickly; he usually talks nonchalantly as he straps it back on. In combat, he'll use it as a club.					
True Spells:		None.			
MenH Items:		None.			
Wealth:		5 Lahavian Dukes (gold)			

Hearing that foreigners have arrived, Bandy Gall will be most pleased to talk to someone "new" and learn all the gossip from them. At the same time, he will endeavor to relieve the players of some coin for anything they'd like to know (about Lahavia or what's north of the Graywall) or do (in Midtown, which has, among other "criminal" enterprises, a hefty prostitution business. This kind demeanor changes as soon as the gruff First Horse has arrived. So the players would be wise to exploit Bandy Gall's greedy kindness as much as possible before then.

Let players chat with Bandy and have a look see in Midtown until you feel that it's time First Horse should arrive with his band of Graymen (on horseback through the north Midtower gate, as they will have gotten back from patrolling).

If the players had insisted to venture out the north gate before his return (against Bandy's advice), they might meet up with some vicious animals or Arkadians shapeshifted into animals. They might even get shot at by First Horse's men, as the forest north of the wall here are quite thick.

Bandy can sell them mundane supplies, hugely over-priced, and none of the weapons are as good as what the players have.

When you introduce First Horse, it's best to have First Horse catch them in a compromising position where they are immediately embarrassed (this could be in Midtown in a house of prostitution, or perhaps they are stealing from Bandy's stash, or whatever...but this will help you to make First Horse the asshole he's supposed to be). First Horse knows they are foreigners and not exiles sent to the Wall, but he will treat them as if they are, initially anyway.

FIRST HORSE: HARD TO IMPRESS, HARD TO PLEASE, STERN					
PHQ	5	TAC	1	MResist: 2d10g +	1d10+8
PHL	2	SOC	2	PResist: 2d10g +	2d10+12
AGL	3	CBT	2	Awareness:	1d10
COR	2	END	1	MTAP:	180
INT	2	ART	1	SK:Bows	R5
INS	3	MYS	1	SK:Long Blades	R3
WIL	5	BV	180	SK:Dodge	R4
EMP	2	DV	10	Other Primary Skills:	R2
MAF	1	MVT	5	Synergy	154
ORank=4 (Warrior/Starborn Lahavian): +12 LUCK (one roll per day), Talents: AGL5:Eyes are Quicker, AGL5:Hands are Quicker, AGL10:Sure Dodge, CBT10:Combat Balloon, COR10:Double Arrow, CBT25:Battle Focus					
True Spells:		None.			
MenH Items: Winter's Heart		Bow: B=25L +5 Primary, +1d5 Secondary			
Wealth:		15 Lahavian Dukes, 150 Roman Aurae (gold)			

Introducing First Horse...

The man that is obviously First Horse is old for a Lahavian, sporting a thick gray beard that loses itself in the fur of his heavy sagum — silver-backed bear, by the looks of it. He just stares at you, picking his teeth clean with an arrow. His bow is still around his shoulder, so it doesn't look like he wants to shoot you, yet. His horse stands at least a hand taller than all the others and seems to be war-trained. He looks at you with disgust in his blue-gray eyes, and then spits a heavy hocker which lands with a splat close to your feet.

"Well boys, what do we have here? Fresh meat lookin' ta help us in our wall duties? You!" — he points at one of the player's characters [choose!] with the arrow he was using to pick his teeth before he spit — what did you do ta piss off ole Maudine, that pretty Grand Duchess o'mine, look at'er tits?

If the players make any aggressive move, First Horse and the rest of the Graymen (7 in all, ORank=1 Warriors), nock their arrows and you can call REACTION to start Phase Combat. First Horse wants nothing more than to ridicule them, relieve them of some coin and send them on their way, but he also loves to scrap. He won't try to kill them, but he will teach the players a lesson in humility...

If the players choose instead to banter, First Horse gladly

accepts any cut-downs as jokes, and dishes more out himself, tempting combat until he gets that the players aren't there to show how powerful they are. Then, he'll move to the next phase: extortion:

"Brady, git down of-a-yer horse an' show these foreigners here some manners." First Horse barks the command out completely ignoring the conversation you were having before. A young La-havian grayman, about 20, dismounts, takes his small gray wool hat off and starts approaching you with it upside down. First Horse talks all the while.

"*You see, whenever foreigners come a-knockin at our Wall, what, you know they always need to bring a gift for my beautiful ole Maudine. After all, she's got to eat, right? Got to keep her plump figure so as to be beautiful to all her graymen that'r keepin' the dangers north of the Wall. So don't be stingy now, gents. And if you be wantin' that we escort you, Mallory here will git down offa his horse and collect a second go-round for our services. What do ya say?*"

Either way, First Horse collects an offering (even if he has to fight them for it), and then brings them to Bandy Gall to resupply and perhaps get stitched up (there is no magical healing they can offer, unless you think Bandy might have a couple potions or healing salves he'll charge them for).

In First Horse's presence, Bandy tries to act tough and demeaning towards the players and always agrees with First Horse about *anything* First Horse says. It is easy to see who the real "governor" here is, and it isn't Bandy.

Still, First Horse plays the role, and asks Bandy for "permission" to do anything, including escort (if that was opted for) the foreigners north of the wall.

[If you want to show the players more of Lahavia, you're more than welcome to take them west to Ice Tower and bring them into Arkadia by way of Snowmantle, a hidden Celtic village where they can meet Horace Pargol, a druid. Or, you can replace Midtown/Midtower with Ice Town and Ice Tower. Horace Pargol, though ornery, will help them understand the Arkadian ways and ensure they don't disrespect the land or the spirits. See *Dawn of the Seventh Age* (Book 4 of the Immortal Empires novels) to see how to role-play Horace Pargol.]

North into Pictland & Arkadia

If you like, you can send a band of vicious Picts, covered in blue paint, at them and have an encounter. First Horse's men will fight the Picts to the death, if First Horse has been hired to escort them. We'll leave it to you to draw up the Pict's stats. After about eight hours of horseback walking north, read them this:

The cold sinks deeper into your bones the further north you go. The trek is slow, as the forest is thick. You can hardly imagine how it would be if you went off the path. You can hardly imagine how anyone could survive out here, where it was winter all year long. But the birds chirping show that it is possible, as long as you are cold-blooded.

But you suddenly realize, the birds are no longer chirping, and you cannot remember how long ago they stopped. There's nothing but the hiss of wind through the evergreens. And then, you hear on the wind a voice, a whisper. In your own language it says, "Turn back or suffer our fate you shall." Just beyond the evergreens in front of you, you see what appears to be paradise: green, lush vegetation and all manner of trees bearing fruit at least three times the normal size.

Give the players a moment to consider and prepare.

If First Horse is with them, he just keeps riding forward, but the other graymen turn back, they and their horses spooked. They dare not go further. First Horse will lead them to the natural boundary between Pictland and Arkadia, a small river separating the harsh wintry cold and evergreens on the south from the beautiful green and lush land with trees bearing huge fruits to the north.

If First Horse is with them, he will tell them they ought to ask permission of the Arkadian spirits to enter. Showing respect in Arkadia goes a long way to keeping yourself healthy, he'll say. If they didn't hire him, they'll have to defeat a water elemental to get across the small river. First Horse will not cross the river.

Water Elemental: Force 3 Lesser (SC106):3000exp

If they don't ask permission to enter Arkadia (a silent response means that permission is granted), then they will have to defeat the Spirit of the Grove as well:

Corporeal Spirit: Glory 2 Lesser (SC107):2000exp

Of course, the Green Man (or an Arkadian shapeshifted into an animal of any sort) will be watching all of this. The more disrespectful the players are to Arkadia, the harder it will be for them to find the Greenman or a talking animal (an Arkadian).

However, if they are repentant (even though they may have killed the elemental, the spirit, or even a shapeshifted Arkadian kraal warrior), they will succeed in finding someone to help them.

A **krall warrior** of any vicious animal type should have something close to this statline: 2:2/022/444/337:1240exp.

Arkadia

As you know from the Storyteller's Codex, Arkadia is a magical land flowing with milk and honey and everything in between. However, at the time in this Adventure, the fey have not yet returned (being trapped in the Cave of Dreams ever since the Original Coven used blood magic at Antara's and He Who Stands Alone's suggestion to create the prison for the Marunes.

Not only did every fey in the world get trapped, but also every Marune except He Who Stands Alone (at that time, HWSA cared not a whit about Those Who Run Together, so he made sure all of them were either in the World or in the Dreamscape in order that they be trapped as well).

The fey who exist in Faerie Realm (a pocket Dimension) were not affected, but portals to and from Faerie Realm were also sealed, coinciding with the seal placed on the Cave of Dreams to close it. The implications of this you should be able to extrapolate: there were Arkadians (perhaps other races, including wicked Blood Shamans) in Faerie Realm when it was sealed, who might be powerful immortal Greater Archons by now, as Faerie Realm time is different than the world's. Additionally, there are probably many untamed fey (monsters) who, considering the great lack of Arkadian Faerie Lords in Faerie Realm, no longer fear Arkadians or immediately obey their commands. This is all important when your players succeed in opening the Cave of Dreams in this Adventure, unsealing both the Cave and the Faerie Realm portals.

(We should add here also that the Wyrmkyn were created of every Ancient Race as a by-product of proximity to the ultra-powerful spell, and that the dragons disappeared a split second before the Cast of Woes, and so were not trapped by that spell. Also, make a point about dead white birch trees everywhere.)

So, getting back to our main point about the state of Arkadia in this Adventure's time. Arkadia is indeed still scattered throughout the world as small magical zones in remote places, the largest of these being the beautiful lands north of Pictland. While there are no fey (and also no fey animals), there are Arkadians shapeshifted as such, especially those shapeshifted into monstrous animals of legend. By these frightful means, they aim to keep Arkadia pure and uninhabited by other races until the return of their fey armies.

They feel they must use this tactic because Arkadians, though the first born Ancient Race, are the least fertile of them all, and therefore the least in population size. Without their massive fey armies, they are easily conquerable by any other Ancient Race which might foray unchecked with that intention.

Hence, it widely believed (except among the highest elites like Optimus Verus, Aunt Julia, and some other immortals), that the Arkadians also disappeared with the creation of the Cave of Dreams back at the end of the First Age.

Your players should thus believe that too, at the outset (and so the player who is to later role-play the Arkadian "Elemental Spirit" coven member should probably be shapeshifted into a different race, unbeknown to them.

Arkadia is magical. There must be shown a respect for nature therein for the magical land to welcome them. If disrespect is shown, the magical land will fight them at every turn, sending mosquitoes instead of butterflies, thorns instead of carnations, and so on. The more evil they do, the more they will reap. And all this is in addition to what the Arkadian Watchers themselves will witness and accuse the players of.

You'll have to be careful with this, because many players always want to roll their REACTION and start showing how wonderfully badass they are. And, unfortunately, the Arkadians won't play: they kill, because they're protecting their homeland at all costs until the return of the fey.

Thus, it's best to let them come across a Blood Shaman before they get into too much trouble with the Arkadians and the magical Arkadia itself. That way, their "trigger happy" members can enjoy themselves while at the same time helping to defend Arkadia from Wyrmkyn or Blood Shaman invaders.

Finally, the journey in Arkadia culminates in the Hidden Vale, the Heart of Arkadia, where they learn that the Power, Arkadi Orkani, is in the world. She will reward them according to their conduct on their journey there.

BLOOD SHAMAN: RUTHLESS, SECRETIVE, PSYCHOTIC					
PHQ	1	TAC	1	MResist: 2d10g +	2d10+6
PHL	3	SOC	0	PResist: 2d10g +	1d10+2
AGL	3	CBT	1	Awareness:	1d10
COR	2	END	2	MTAP:	310
INT	4	ART	1	SK:Casting	R2
INS	3	MYS	2	SK:Short Blades	R1
WIL	3	BV	200	SK:Dodge	R1
EMP	0	DV	7	Other Primary Skills:	R2
MAF	4	MVT	4	Synergy	73
				MCTRL:	24m/48S/72M

ORank=2 (Sorcerer/Starborn Celt): +2 LUCK (one roll per day), Talents: Use Pure Negative energy as Source, MAF0:Master Scholar's Lock, INT5:Catachresis, INT10:Banausic Mind	
True Spells:: See Appendix	Shaman Drain, Shaman Bloodletting, Shaman Charm, Shaman Bloodfire
MenH Items: Rat Skull Ring	B=15L Tertiary Focus: CUR/OFF/UTL Magic
Magical Access:	M: UTL/CUR, S:CHA/OFF, m:CON/DEF

When you're ready for the Blood Shaman Encounter...have the players roll their Awareness. Any TN15 or higher yields:

The melody of the birds no longer accompanies your brave trek into the untamed jungles of Arkadia, but a sweet aroma does. With every step, it gets stronger, and it smells like grilled rabbit!

The Blood Shaman's campfire is obscured by the jungle vegetation, and the Blood Shaman is out collecting more firewood at the moment of their arrival. If they wait quietly, they'll be able to catch the Blood Shaman unawares (gaining surprise). Of course, they might not know that this is a very evil blood-magic casting servant of a Marune Minion who has sent her to bring back the blood of an Arkadian kraal warrior for some sinister purpose, but they might be able to role their SK:Lore:Arcane TN15 to surmise that this is a blood shaman.

If engaged in friendly talk, the Shaman will be distrustful and endeavor to charm one of the party in an attempt to kill them all (Ancient Race blood is more powerful than animal blood).

If they approach to see the campfire, a silent alarm will warn the Blood Shaman that someone (or an animal) has entered her camp. She will hasten to return, but with caution.

In this very small clearing you find two small rabbits on a roasting stick over a medium fire that obviously needs more wood to keep going. Hanging upside down on ten more poles are the carcasses of twenty more rabbits draining bright red blood into a hollowed out log trough about eight feet from end to end. There's no tent, no sleeping arrangements, but it looks like the owner is currently away.

Obviously, 22 rabbits is overkill to feed just one or two people (and any SK:Tracking shows there is just one person: TN10). Also, it's standard to bleed food dry before cooking, but saving it in a log trough? Hmmm. Something is just not right about this.

Blood Shamans always save blood from animals (+5/die Potency)(and humans, if possible (+10/die Potency)) whenever they stop or travel, for their own protection. Remember that use of Blood Magic kills vegetation and small animals in as many Hexes Radius as Potency d10s rolled (so Open-Ended 10s would increase the radius), so be sure to visualize this to the players if it happens; it is a huge sin to cast blood magic in Arkadia, and incurs the death penalty.

If the party has figured out that this wanderer is an enemy and attacks, the first spell the Shaman will attempt is her Bloodfire, mingling the blood from the trough with the fire roasting her rabbits. The blood rises up, swirls through and mixes with the fire and then shoots out to each of the party members that are in the area (see Appendix for the TrueSpells used by Personalities in this Adventure).

If made to talk, the Blood Shaman readily calls the Arkadians liars and deceivers, that they do exist, and have lied to the whole world all this time. If pressed, she will attempt to make a deal for her life or for the blood of an Arkadian "prince" in return for any favor she can bestow.

If you want to get really nasty with the party, you could always have the Blood Shaman use some Blood Magic to give unlife to the rabbits (who would chew themselves down from the poles in a second). Then the zombie rabbits would attack the party, but you'll have to be familiar with Overbearing Rules (SC177). We recommend zombie rabbits, especially if the Blood Shaman is away and the party has ventured into the camp uninvited.

Ultimately, the safest course for the party is just to kill the Blood Shaman, especially if you have it such that a shapeshifted Arkadian has been monitoring the party's movement and conduct.

Simcha and Queen Brûd

Somehow or another, they will run into Simcha, Queen Brûd's wandering sister. She can appear as any animal, but her favorite is a sexy black panther. If the party has done well against the Blood Shaman, perhaps she will reveal herself to them.

If they bargained with the Blood Shaman, Simcha will go kill the Blood Shaman first and then come to bring the Party to Judgment, using her Arkadian Animal Forms (as a R9 Greater Archon) to bring each of them to unconsciousness, in order to bring them to her sister for judgment.

Either way, the party will make it to Queen Brûd's throne where they will have to answer as to why they are in Arkadia, in addition to rendering excuses for all their unacceptable conduct while in Arkadia.

If they have indeed sinned (and perhaps one or more of them deserves The Ingrate's Retribution (AR178) curse placed on them), they will have to do one additional step while in the Hidden Vale, and that would be to ascend the Ivory Tower and beg Arkadi Orkani's forgiveness.

Supposing they convincingly explain themselves (and don't forget to show Queen Brûd the little scroll they were given), they will receive hospitality, including magical healing (even if they incurred a curse), food and shelter, while the Queen discusses their fate with the other matrons.

After studying each party member with The Unveiling, Queen Brûd sees that they all have Favored by Antara in their auras. Could these five be the Original Coven reincarnated? There's only one way to find out: to send them to the Hidden Vale in search of the Original Elements. If they find them, and the Original Elements do not reject them, then perhaps Antara's Prophecy (and the whole story behind it will be shared as they sit around a large village fire) is actually coming true, at last!

Note: the Arkadians will not teach the party DreamCarver.

Admin Time

Now would be a good time to award Experience Points and Fortune Points, and help each player increase their ORanks, spend their X-Pts on their Attributes, spend their Fortune Points increasing Skill ranks, and so on.

A properly run admin session for 5 players is fun and can take an hour or more. They should have taken notes (as you should have) on what great, and what idiotic, things they did. Having a pissing contest with First Horse and getting the crap beat out of them would probably earn a great big fat goose egg (ZERO) for experience points.

But somehow tricking the greedy Bandy Gall out of some of his coin might have earned 500 or even 1000, depending on the role play involved. Simple thing is: the players have to come up with reasons they deserve an award; if they cannot remember what their characters did, why should anyone else? Every player can help each other remember, and you should not be stingy with group awards for when they all worked together.

Hopefully, you've placed enough challenges in their way up to this point to get them to have a party average of ORank=3, since that is what this next section will be based on.

THE VILLAGE CAMPFIRE

Now that the players know that Arkadians *are* in the world, and that all the stories of vicious, monstrous animals were really about shapeshifted Arkadians defending their homeland, they're in even more danger of being killed by the Arkadians so that Queen Brûd can keep their secret safe.

But one thing [and one thing alone] holds her back, and it isn't the handwritten plea from Empress Maximina. It's the possibility that these four adventurers (five if there are five) might be reincarnations of the Original Coven. Queen Brûd knows the prophecy quite well, as it has been their hope for Ages, that the Original Coven will once again find each other and open the Cave of Dreams, and in doing so, free all the fey from that dreadful place.

So, Queen Brûd agrees to help the party, but is not completely honest with them about where and why they have to go. She knows exactly where the entrance to the Cave of Dreams is, but she must know for certain if this is the Coven reincarnated. If they aren't, they'll fail, and she'll care not a whit about any of them, and not even about Maximina's concern for her brother.

Also, now that the players are feeling pretty good that their characters have gained a few Ranks and are more powerful, it's the perfect time for you to tell the Story of the Cave of Dreams. They will have the rare privilege of meeting the immortal and wise King Halon of the Arkadians who has been alive since the First Age. It is he who will tell the story. So, at the behest of Queen Brûd, Halon begins his story...

The old immortal reluctantly stands and rebukes the Queen, "Alright, alright, stop your prodding. You're getting to be worse than Evlain with all your demands! You'd think that after five or six thousand years a man could decide on his own whether he wanted to sit or stand to talk or be silent!" His modern Astorian is quite good for a people who have cut themselves off from the rest of the world, and it seems that all the other Arkadians in the village understand it very well too, since they laugh at his ornery scolding.

For her part, Queen Brûd merely glares at him, obviously not finding anything funny in what he said. After he turns away from her to address your group, she closes her eyes as if meditating.

King Halon jerks his long white warrior's braid hard, as if that is what he would do to her, he winces at the self-inflicted pain, and again, the younger Arkadians laugh, especially the children, who even at ages five or six have their first kill tattoos already on them. You can tell that Halon is greatly loved by all, even, if you caught it, the Queen, who had opened one eye to see him look over his shoulder at her when the children laughed. Was that the crack of a smile on her face? But now, Halon begins in earnest.

"Back a long, long time ago, when I was just a young man with a nice dark but short warrior's braid full of jade, rubies, and love trinkets from various Arkadian admirers wishing to steal me away from Evlain, there began a commotion in a small village I called

home. You know, back then, women were just as gossipy as now with all their meddling and plotting, but the arguing became so great that the men had to step in just to keep the peace."

A small Arkadian girl interrupts Halon, "Grandfather, what were they arguing about?"

"Well, I'll tell you, young one. You see, those evil Marunes were going about killing off dragons and fey with their mere presence. Whenever they didn't like the offering we were forced to send to them, they'd just kill off our friends."

"But The Pact," a boy of about twelve answered.

"The Pact only protects the Ancient Races, not our friends. The Marunes are free to strike our friends whenever they see fit, but cannot harm us unless we harm them first. That is why we are called Faerie Lords, because we fulfilled the role as their protectors. So the argument was that the Greater Coven should cast a great spell, creating an indestructible Prison on the Dreamscape that would trap all the Marunes in it for all ages to come. But, in order for it to work, Antara said that the spell must contain the blood of the Marunes."

"Blood Magic?" yet another child asked.

"Yes, my young kraal warrior, Blood Magic! Of course, we knew full well that Blood Magic kills, and such a great spell, cast in our greatest Place of Power, our own Mor Z'Pyr, our great Wyrmtree, might have devastating consequences. But proponents of the spell, namely the Astorians and their wicked King Tarchon, who was willingly deceived by his Cloud Dragons, insisted that it was the only way to free the world from the grip of the Marunes.

"Our own people decided under Evlain that we were against the Casting of Blood Magic. But the Synod of the Ancient Races voted for it. We immediately went to war with the Astorians. But there was not enough time even for the first battle to be decided. The Original Coven, began to cast the spell, with Antara hovering over them. Clouds rolled in with thunder and lightning. The winds blew angrily, swirling around our Wyrmtree.

"Truly, it was an amazing, if terrifying, sight. The Coven, seated on five red crystal thrones, each of them, hovering above the Wyrmtree in a circle, with our Arkadian sister, Boreas, at the center, speaking the ominous words of what became known as the Cast of Woes. Around her sat the other Original Coven members: Achernar the Astorian (Air), Malekbel the Ammorian (Fire), Karfyn the Atlantean (Water), and Arumbrek the Oshekogan (Earth).

"My dragon, yes, I had a Companion back then. Hard to believe, I know, that I could be worthy of one of the Great Ones, but my dragon warned me to skedaddle. So, just as Antara was getting ready to pour the Marune blood into the mix of original elements the in the bowl Boreas held, I and my dragon fled. When I arrived safely in the Hidden Vale, but alone. My Companion was nowhere to be found. I could have died that day for that loss.

"I sensed the world had changed. My bonds with my Companion and several Faerie rulers were gone. Arkadia seemed broken,

weaker. I journeyed back to Mor Z'Pyr only to find that the great Wyrmtree that was at the center of our nations was dead, the top half and its beautiful canopy gone, as if it had exploded like a volcano. Only the lower trunk was left. The land was warped and different.

"Indeed, the Cast of Woes trapped not only the Marunes (all except that wily chief of them, He Who Stands Alone), but also all the faeries, and to the best of our knowledge, all the Great Wyrms as well. We walked the Dreamscape to discover that indeed The Great Citadel, that horrible prison that manifested there and in the earth as The Cave of Dreams, was indeed created. But at what great cost!

"Seeing her own failure and immediately repentant, Antara at once was determined to reverse the error. Taking deceitful counsel from the sole surviving Marune, she believed the only way to reverse the Cast of Woes was to murder the entire Original Coven, thinking that it would cancel the magic they had cast.

"Antara hunted each coven member down, one by one, stole from them the Original Elements, and slaughtered them, not without tears in her eyes. The last to be found was Karfyn the Atlantean, whom she killed by trapping in a massive amount of ice, since he was keeping her at bay by commanding the water around him to push her to the other side of the world.

"In her sorrow, she took an oath: 'For these five lives that today ye must give, I shall cause ye each five more to live.' And thus was born the prophecy that somehow, the Original Coven reincarnated would find a way to open the Cave of Dreams and free the fey trapped in it, and then our White Birch trees would then come back to life, happy that the fey are returned.

"Antara took the five Original Elements and hid them. We all know where, and that is why we call it The Hidden Vale, not because so much that the Vale is hidden, although it is hard to find if you're not an Arkadian, thanks to our Greater Elementals that guard the area, but because the Original Elements are hidden there.

"Later, we found Antara with her head chopped off, with the telltale Immortal rot that only a Marune blade can impose.

"And she's been crazy ever since!" a boy of seven was quick to add. On his arm was a tattoo of a wild boar, a fine, but dangerous kill for such a young boy.

"That's enough, Halon," Queen Brûd interrupted. Halon looked as if he was about to say more, but obeyed and sat back down on a cushion to the right of the Queen's wooden throne. Looking sternly at you, she says:

"You all must go to the Hidden Vale and see if the Spirit Tree will talk to you, tell you where the entrance to the Cave of Dreams is on this world. The ancient paths are no doubt hidden after so many years. Only then will you be able to help your Empress and her brother and receive the reward they have promised. My own sister, Simcha, shall select the group of warriors who shall lead you to the Hidden Vale, but once there, they cannot help you. You must rise or fall on your own merits. It is the way of our people, and, it is

the way of the Cave of Dreams. Gather your strength and rest, for the journey before you is long and arduous are the trials at its end."

With this, Queen Brûd will get up off of her throne and go into her hut. Her decree has been uttered and she has nothing more to say.

You should arrange a couple of encounters along the way with unwelcome foreigners who have penetrated into Arkadia in order to steal its blessed fruit seeds and large animal skins/furs. They need not be Blood Shamans, but they should give the players a challenge, especially because they have additional help with their Arkadian escort.

Some of the escort might die in these encounters, which is perfectly fine. It might reinforce how dangerous this whole mission is. The escort, in the meantime, will speak freely of the Hidden Vale, and also of the dangers of the Black Forest which is part of that Vale. It's up to you how much knowledge you want your players to have about it.

If it looks like one of the player's characters is about to die, Simcha will shoot an arrow from hiding that will pierce the would-be killer's throat. It's Brûd's order that the group makes it alive to the Hidden Vale. You need not reveal that Simcha is watching over them; it will be enough to know that the arrow mysteriously saved their life...

We suggest you create enemies for the group to fight that are slightly higher in ORank and skills so that the experience will be more. Also, you might want to let them have a couple of MenH items they'll take off their fallen enemies. Each of the trials in the Hidden Vale is dangerous, especially the one in the Black Forest. So prepare them well, but keep it a challenge.

The Hidden Vale

While she will not interfere, the powerful Simcha will secretly track and monitor all the players' progress and report everything hourly back to Brûd, who will have dispatched four Kraal and one Vale Warrior (their captain, a female) to escort the party to the Hidden Vale. The escort can freely go into the Hidden Vale, but they will merely set up camp and not interfere with any of the players' interactions therein. Not even should they meddle with the Wyrm eggs. Everything concerning the prophecy of the Original Coven must work without their intervention for it to become true, they fully believe.

There are five tests in the Hidden Vale, and successful navigation of each allows them to gain the Original Element for that test. By now, you should be able to assign the Original Elements to the proper character in the way they have been role-played: Fire = short-tempered and brash, destructive, consuming; Water = flowing, graceful, yet powerful and unrelenting; Air = Silent, hidden, but wise and all-seeing, the voice of reason; Earth = rugged, tough, dirty, strong, loyal, a healer; Spirit = emotional, trusting, truthful, contemplative, and caring about the others.

The entire land of Hidden Vale is a Force 5 Greater Earth Elemental (Base Form). The lake in the center of the vale that surrounds the Wyrm's Isle is a Force 5 Greater Water Elemental (also in Base Form). The air is, yup, you guessed it, a Force 5 Greater Air Elemental. If anyone dives deep enough, they will see that at the bottom of the lake is where the fire is (yup: F5 Greater).

These elementals protect the Hidden Vale from destruction, but they don't mind if someone wants to drink the water or dig or breathe the air.

The Arkadians consider the Hidden Vale 'holy ground' and refuse to kill anyone or anything on it, entrusting that to the paragon elementals that guard the place. They know that the Alabaster Tower at the center of the Geode Isle is where Arkadi Orkani resides (when she is incarnate, in the flesh) as a spirit of considerable Glory. If any of the party has been cursed with the Ingrate's Retribution and wants to atone, they must enter the tower and seek her forgiveness, and that all depends on how they acted after they were cursed. That is all the Arkadian guides will tell them.

IMPORTANT. At this point, you should know:

[1] In STORY only (meaning not on their character records), the players' characters transform INTO the Original Coven after they find all of the Original Elements. Give them copies of the Original Coven Character Records in the Appendix to play. In the Story, the players' characters still have memories of their life and name, but now also have the foggy memories of the Original Coven member of whom they are a reincarnation. At any obstacle, they may role a new skill to help them overcome: SK:Lore:-Original Coven.

[2] As soon as the Original Elements convert them into the Original Coven Member (which will only happen when all of the Original Elements are found so it happens to all of them at once), each Coven Member receives a vision of the Bonded Warrior attached to them. Each then has a choice to accept their Bonded Warrior or to go it alone. If they accept, then their current Character Record (along with their current ORank and stats) becomes the Bonded Warrior's Character Record and they can choose a new name for this character. The Bonded Warrior steps into reality from the pocket Dimension which the Original Element is.

[3] Each player, then, will have to role-play both the Coven Member (from the Appendix) and the Bonded Warrior. In any case, they will need a minimum of the stats and abilities listed on the Coven's Character Records in order to successfully complete the Adventure...so...

If you want to just add all of these abilities (and increase their ORank, etc. to that of the Character Records in the Appendix) then you can have them transform without any mention of Bonded Warriors (and let the Arkadians that escorted them to the Hidden Vale become their Bonded Warriors as Personalities that YOU control. This option would be most beneficial to a more inexperienced *group of players who can barely keep track of the one character they have. You may need an Admin Session to get all of this done; the method we suggested in [1]-[3] helps you to avoid the Admin Session, as all you have to do is hand out the Original Coven character records.*

It is all-important in this Adventure that the Original Coven members survive all the way to the red crystal throne room in the Cave of Dreams, but you can't cheese it or make it easy for them. If they fail, let them know they failed and that's the end: obviously they weren't the true reincarnations of the Original Coven. Then, you have the option of letting them roll up new characters (who were also hired and sent by Optimus or Maximillian in the same manner their old characters were...so it's possible their new character arrives at the Hidden Valley just as their old character dies (we know...and we just said not to cheese it, but...hopefully none of them dies so that you have to face this type of scenario!)

The Elemental Trials of Antara

In order to ensure no one but the reincarnated Coven Members are able to obtain the Original Elements, Antara created these trials. If the players become stuck and cannot figure something out, you might want to remind them via SK:Lore:Original Coven that these tests have a great deal to do with every element: a test for Spirit, a test for Fire, for Earth, for Water, and for Air.

You are free to give them other helps/hints as well, and to modify damage they might take if our general scenario is too powerful for their ORank (since we do not know exactly what ORank your players will be).

THE HIDDEN VALE

As soon as you crest the small mountain into what your guides tell you is the Hidden Vale, your pent-up excitement fades to disappointment. The whole valley is barren except for the impenetrable forest of Black Birch trees on the far side. To your left is a broken down water mill whose wheel refuses to turn, even under the weight of the small waterfall pouring into it. To your right, a dilapidated rath that looks like an abandoned fort. In the center of all this is a large lake of standing water and mosquitoes which surrounds an island of ugly geodes. At the center of that geode-island stands a hundred-foot high weathered tower of alabaster, multiple cracks threatening to tumble it to the geodes below.

It's hard to believe that the exalted Original Coven lived in this unimpressive vale, which bears absolutely no resemblance to the rest of the blessed and magical lands the form Arkadia.

The Arkadian guides will set up camp and leave the Party to their own designs. They will not meddle, nor will they answer any questions about anything in this vale.

The Party is free to do the trials in any order, but hopefully they choose to do the Black Forest last (and after an Admin Session, so their odds of survival are greater). It is the most daunting of the tests.

Spirit's Rath - SPIRIT (Part 1)

Once a small but magnificent structure, the rath is now barely more than ruins. There is still a door, however, and an inside chamber that is only accessible through that door, it appears. On either side of the door is a hemispherical fountain bowl. Each appears to have caught some rainwater, as the fountains have long since stopped pouring from the looks of it.

Drinking from the left fountain pool makes a person go blind. Drinking from the right does nothing (unless you are blind, and then it bestows a temporary Spirit Sight to the person).

Anyone can easily enter the rath to find five statues on either side of a stone hall that leads to a broken stone throne. With spirit sight, they will notice five of the statues glowing (it matters not which), and that the throne is empty and not glowing.

The statues on the throne's right are those of the Original Coven. The statues on the throne's left are all warriors of one race or another. By the way they are facing and staring at the Original Coven statues, one could guess that these are the Bonded Warriors.

If any of the statues or throne is touched, all five spirits will attack the whole group, whoever is inside the rath (and this throne room is the only room).

Rath Spirit Guards: F2 Lesser Incorporeal (Restless Shamed)

They will be invisible to anyone without Spirit Sight. They can only be damaged by MenH-L/g weapons or spells, and they attack first every Phase. Anyone with Spirit Sight can dodge their attacks and target them normally, but without Spirit Sight these spirits can only be hit on a CRIT1-5 and cannot be dodged. The spirits will attempt to chase the intruders out of the rath.

These spirits are not the spirits of the Bonded Warriors, but only the guards of the rath who failed to protect Lady Spirit from Antara.

This is only *part* of the test for Spirit (and the Original Element Spirit is not here). Anyone who sits in the throne (after vanquishing/freeing the Restless Shamed trapped here) will feel an immense sorrow and instantly know the reason all the White Birch trees along the Arkadian Leylines are dead: their power was used by Antara to kill Lady Spirit (Boreas). The throne sitter/toucher will be overcome by Elemental Spirit: Sorrow, and not want to leave the throne, thinking all is worthless, unless he rolls a MResist greater than 75. The other party members will have to pull him/her off. As soon as there is no contact with the throne, the elemental spirit effect no longer applies.

At the moment of death (being freed, actually), each Restless Shamed spirit will be so happy that they finally received justice at the hands of what they "know" to be the Coven Reincarnated, that they linger (as they receive glory and corporeal form) to answer any questions (one question each) that the party might have, especially about the Black Forest...

Under the Lake - WATER!

The light of the sky fades as you delve deeper into the lake. Darkness was just about to swallow you up until an orange glow further down just came into view. Strange, the water seems warmer down here, when it should be ice cold this deep.

At the bottom of the lake (about 1,000 feet down, so they will either need to Shapeshift or summon an Air Elemental or use Utility magic to help them breathe), they will see that the entire bottom is covered in a magical fire (as it is not lava). This fire is a F5 Greater fire elemental.

As long as the Elemental is not attacked (with a magical weapon that is of a Greater Binding), it will not radiate a killing heat. It is warm only, and can easily be passed through without harm. Hidden underneath the fire is a huge disk of ice (Awareness TN30 / TAC TN20 to notice the ice disk through the fire if *in* the fire; if not in the fire then the TNs are one category higher).

If TNs are reached, they will know it's obviously a round disk (about 1000 feet in diameter). If they search out the center, they'll find that there is a person trapped in the center of the ice. Upon close inspection, this person is an Ancient Atlantean, and could possibly be (it is) the Original Coven member Karfyn. The ice is impenetrable, and only the F5 Fire Elemental is powerful enough to melt it (which it will refuse to do unless somehow the players roll a CRIT:5 in magically commanding the elemental to do so).

However, the body in the ice is dead, and therefore has no Magic Resistance. The 100% answer would be to use Divination magic to Divine on the body and then Travel magic to Travel it Through Divination. The Original Element (Water) will cling to the body and then roll onto one of the party members touching the body they rescued. If the party tries to Travel the body without first using Divination (to bypass the magic resistance of the Ice), they will have to overcome the Ice Disk's binding of B=20g (or B=100L).

Storyteller » IT IS IMPORTANT THAT AT LEAST ONE OF THE PLAYERS HAVE GREATER ACCESS TO THE TRAVEL SCHOOL IN ORDER TO SOLVE THIS PUZZLE. GUIDE THEM APTLY IN ADMIN SESSION

The interesting thing about this challenge is that the players are able to use Divination to talk with Karfyn's spirit, since they have both a Body and Place of Death to use as Major Gateways. Karfyn's spirit (Glory 5g) will not resist being summoned (especially if the party member who is his reincarnation, since one cannot resist his own magic). He can tell them much, including his wish that they bury his remains in The Final Resting Place under Arkadi Orkani's alabaster tower. Since he was the last Original Coven Member to be killed by Antara, he will be able to tell them the whole story, and how he fled to hide from her way down here, trying to use the water to keep her away. He is wholly convinced that she is a psychopath.

THE WATER MILL - EARTH

As you approach the Mill, the sound of the waterfall gets louder, but as it crashes with great force down into the buckets of the large water wheel, the wheel budges not an inch. The mill and the wheel are built of wood, walnut, from its hue. The wheel must be Magically Enhanced for it to have lasted this long under the water. But the mill structure itself doesn't appear to be so favored, with its broken supports and joists. The extent of the damage done to the millstones and floor speak of more violence than mere weathering can do, however, as if an earthquake somehow tore the mill apart while leaving the wheel completely intact and in place.

Upon closer inspection, fresh, ungrounded wheat spills out of broken storage vats in a large barn-like (warehouse) chamber next to the millstones. There is no "weathering" in the Hidden Valley. There is enough wheat here to feed the entire Arkadian population for decades, and probably enough to feed all of the Astorian Empire for a whole month. Each month, the Arkadians have gathered grain and made offerings in honor of their Power, Arkadi Orkani, whose Philosophy they follow.

Anyone is free to eat of the grain, but of course it hasn't been milled into flour because the millstone won't turn. In order to find out why, someone has to dive into the water to see what is going on with the bottom third of the gigantic wheel (the water is indeed the huge lake in this valley).

The bottom of the wheel is embedded in a huge boulder that seems to be growing out of the shore. The wheel is indestructible, and the rock, well, it might as well be for the party:

Quiet Rock: Force 4 Lesser Stone (Earth) Elemental with DV=15 (Special: because of Original Element contact: Earth)

Quiet Rock wants everything to be QUIET so it can sleep to the soothing sound of the waterfall. Unfortunately, the turning wheel generates a lot of noise and rumble (from the millstones) that interferes with this happiness.

The players can try to kill Quiet Rock if they want, but the much easier path is to convince Quiet Rock (who will be able to speak their languages, so old is he), that there is another, more beautiful place to sleep somewhere away from the Mill. This answer can take many forms: a Glimmering of sound leading him away from the waterfall, one of the party members singing a beautiful melody (TN30+ SK:Singing and the trait Pure Voice will definitely help) as she leads him away from the Mill), etc.

In any case, once Quiet Rock leaves the area, the wheel will again turn and the loud noise of the mill will start again (so Quiet Rock will have to be distracted enough not to notice). Quiet Rock was hiding Arumbrek's skeleton in one of the wheel's buck-

ets. If he is convinced that there is a better place elsewhere, Quiet Rock reluctantly leaves his treasure behind (not that it cares for the skeleton, but unbeknown to it, the Original Element (Earth) is there and keeps the elemental feeling full of vitality and life (hence the TN30+ requirement to lead him away from it).

Once parted, Quiet Rock will no longer enjoy the DV=15 benefit from the Original Element.

All the wheel's buckets always hang upright, and so someone will have to look into the bottom-most bucket to find Arumbrek. The Original Element (a teardrop-sized bit of dirt) will roll itself onto that party member who is to become Earth.

THE BLACK FOREST - AIR

Dominating the northern horizon, black birch trees stand tall and so close together that their limbs are barely extant, their trunks instead effecting a wall about one hundred feet high. Only above this do you start to see branches twisting greedily around each other and stretching up another fifty feet to a dark-leafed canopy that surely blocks out all light for whatever creatures might inhabit that forest.

[if any player asks the forest for permission to enter:] *A breathless voice whispers on a slight breeze of air that passes your ears, "It is not yet night and we are thirsty."*

[if a player hovers to look above the canopy:] *Now that you are above the height of the trees, the sight nearly takes your breath away: the Black Forest extends northward farther than you can see, although it stops by the high ridges of land to its east and west.*

[while higher than the canopy, Awareness TN30 or TAC20:] *Up here, some of the black canopy top has a blood red tint. In fact, upon closer inspection (without crossing over the canopy) you see that there are huge splatters of red in all directions as far as you can see, as if the canopy opened up and ate giant eagles that might have been resting on the canopy's near-solid roof of black leaves and twisting, entwined branches.*

A prelude of the blood sacrifice that will be demanded of them at the Cave of Dreams entrance, the only way to get into the Black Forest is to dabble some living animal above the canopy. The canopy opens to receive its food, and while that is going on, the players can slip by (but of course, they'll need to be able to see in the dark). There's a 50% chance that each player will be attacked by a flailing tree branch as they pass through (as long as an animal is being consumed also; 100% chance if no other animal and 1-5 attacking branches).

If they have successfully navigated the other four tests, and have saved this one for last, Simcha will show up with a beautiful horse with wings (not actually a Pegasus, but that is twice as large as any horse any of them have ever seen) while they are inspecting the Black Forest. The horse is not a fey, per se, but it is a fey animal, and paragon of all horses. It cannot speak but it can understand Ancient Arkadian, and its name is Jentha. Simcha also offers the last five White Birch leaves to them, to eat only when they are certain to enter the Black Forest: the leaves double their Body Value and give them Skyborn Eyes for one hour.

[If the players have already passed the Rath test, the guards of the rath will have plenty of knowledge about how Antara used Jentha as a sacrifice in order to open the Black Forest and hide the key to The Final Resting Place. They will also know that the Black Forest is where Antara killed Achernar, whom she tricked into the Black Forest under pretense that the key would open the Cave of Dreams.]

It is possible for the party to partially sacrifice and then Travel Jentha to safety (and the screams of the horse while being scraped and pierced through by the trees will be harrowing). It would be wise for each member of the party to have an Anchored Travel spell that would get them out of the Black Forest and back to the Hidden Vale (or otherwise figure out a way to open the canopy again so that they can escape (perhaps by saving Jentha and using her multiple times, since it might take them a while to find the bones of Achernar, which would be holding the rather large key in his fingers.

At first, the bloodthirsty trees are so excited about their meal (Jentha) that they will ignore who is treading on their roots (there is more space to maneuver far beneath the canopy). If they sacrifice Jentha completely, they have only thirty minutes that the canopy will be open — probably not enough time to search. But they can divine on the key and/or on the bones of Achernar to be able to open the canopy right above him and retrieve what they need.

The Original Element (Air) is invisible (being air), so it would behoove the party to take Achernar's entire skeleton with them (and the key) out of the Black Forest.

The Black Forest trees age more the deeper one goes into the black forest (all the way to a Statline Rank 5 fey. But for this adventure, Achernar is close to the Hidden Valley, and so they are:

Black Forest Tree: 2:0/999/909/909:2340exp.

That statline is per tree. Also, the trees have an immunity to fire and each acts as a magical drain if cast upon: draining 3x the MTAP of the spell used directly on it. It's up to you as to how many trees can attack each party member or how many branches/roots that are 5% each of its Total BV (with the remaining 50% going to the tree's Vitals, its trunk). Obviously it's a very dangerous place, so hopefully they come up with a good plan.

OPTIONAL ENCOUNTER

If the party lingers too long, they'll catch a glimpse of a Blood Shaman, who appears to have the rainbow eyes of a Marune Minion, spying on them. As soon as the Marune Minion realizes he is discovered, he will flee out of the top of the canopy by offering one of his two small captives, both kraal warriors, to the bloodthirsty trees. The other captive he will let loose while flying over the canopy to try to escape as s/he assumes the players will prior-

itize rescuing the young Arkadians over catching him...for now.

They can use this sacrifice to escape and if they're quick enough, snatch the screaming kraal warrior away from the trees before s/he is completely dead.

Doing so will no doubt deserve a reward from Simcha (or Queen Brûd), and of course they will insist that the party goes after the Marune Minion when they have successfully completed the trials. A suitable reward at this point would be to give each of the players the last 4 or 5 leaves from the white birch trees (which heals them fully instantly and then causes their Common Ability BV Heal Rate to be every hour (instead of every day); this effect lasts for 3 days once eaten. But they will be the last of the leaves until the Cave of Dreams is opened and the white birches revived.

As for the Marune Minion, you can have it be the final "Boss" for the Adventure, so have fun custom-creating him (or her) to give the players a challenge. Remember, Marune Minions will be corrupted and have several "Marune Gifts" from their Bargain with whatever Marune turned them (in this case, it would have to be He Who Stands Alone, since he's the only Marune that is not in the Cave of Dreams at this time).

THE GEODE ISLE - FIRE

While this Arkadian valley is rather small compare to others you've seen, the small island in the center of the large lake seems to get much larger as you approach. You also see something that was hidden from you before: lines of white birch trees that curve out from the Alabaster Tower. All of these trees appear dead as they are devoid of their silvery leaves. Covering the entire island are medium-sized geodes which have not been cracked open. There are thousands of them surrounding the tower all the way out to the water, and they are either green or black. You'll have to be careful not to twist your ankle when walking on them, should you dare to touch them with your body.

You get the idea that the entire isle is somehow hallowed ground, but it isn't the geodes that make it that way. No, it's the inerrant feeling that somewhere within the Alabaster Tower is the Final Resting Place where Lady Spirit and maybe even Malekbel (Fire) were killed.

A TAC TN20 will reveal that there are many more green (dead) geodes and black (alive, unhatched) ones. If they know that these are Wyrm eggs, then this ought to be a source of solemnity, perhaps sorrow. They might even know that no dragon has hatched ever since the dragons disappeared with the Cast of Woes.

There is no visible entrance to the Tower. They will have to move the geodes away from the bottom of the tower to find the trapdoor to enter, but touching the live dragon eggs connects them to the Wyrmsong (they won't know what is really going on unless they CRIT on SK:Lore:Dragon) that right now is nightmarish about death and decay. The daydream effect (nightmare) is so terrifying that each living egg touched or walked upon bestows a horrifying vision and +1UFP (Universal Fatigue Penalty to all their rolls/skills). This penalty is cumulative and will not subside until they are made whole with "becoming" the Original Coven and regaining their foggy memories of their past reincarnation(s).

The dead wyrm eggs (the green ones) produce no effect and can be easily cracked open to reveal the multicolor beauty of a crystallized geode.

So, the 100% answer is to use Utility:Levitate (or an Air Elemental) to move the black geodes without touching them. They will have to move at least 30 live eggs and 40 dead eggs in order to open the trapdoor.

As soon as the trapdoor is opened, the underside will reveal at first a skeleton with a beady eye of fire staring at them. Go ahead an call for REACTION, as this might be something trying to attack them.

Of course, it is only Malekbel's skeleton with the Original Element (Fire) swimming around in his skull. If you think the skeleton has been animated with hatred for those who dare disturb the Final Resting Place (or perhaps they touched too many live wyrm eggs, disrespecting them), then the skeleton may well attack them: Malekbel will attack last in every phase and has two hand attacks (claws), a bite, and one kick. If animated, it will not be by power of the Shadowscape, but the Dimension of Brilliance (and as such it will be glowing white with the Original Element (Fire) flaring hot/flames with each attack).

Malekbel's Skeleton: 10/24,59,18/33,10,29/33,10,38:9750exp

Once the skeleton is no longer a threat, the Original Element (Fire) will make its way to that player's character who has been delegated by you to become fire.

The Alabaster Tower - SPIRIT (part 2)

The trapdoor's stairs spiral in and down directly under the tower. There is no light down here. It really does feel like a tomb.

If they have Skyborn Eyes active, then they can see the bottom about 100 feet below them. Otherwise, allow the players to somehow light their path, then continue. If they don't (we had one playtest group Shapeshift into bats) then modify your answer appropriately, based on what you have waiting for them below!

The light helps, but the darkness is to thick you can only see a few feet as the stairs keep spiraling down into darkness. It isn't at all what you would expect from the bright and cheerful Power Arkadi Orkani, who loves life and light and joy and beauty.

At this point, the players should be wondering "how do we get UP to the part of the tower that is above ground!" Upon consideration of this and inspection, assign a Target Number for them to realize (based on their lighting) that the spiral staircase is identical on both sides of the same stair (that is, if you were a vertical mirror image of yourself, you would be seen to be standing on

the underside of the stairs). In fact, if they climb around to the other side, or get to the bottom and attempt to "walk" up the underside of the staircase, gravity will reverse for them so that they can, and that is how they can get up to the above-ground tower levels.

Arkadi Orkani, aka "The Maiden" is the first of a cycle of three ("The Mother" (Antara) and "The Old Crone" (Ash)). She hates all so-called "precious" metals, loves nature and wood and stone. She loves renewal and birth and youth and beauty. She reincarnates, the same as Antara and Ash, in her time, but she rarely ventures beyond the borders of Arkadia, preferring to enjoy, as it were, the Garden of Eden above all the other wonders the world has to offer.

While they might never see her (it is up to you whether she has reincarnated at the time of this Adventure), people can commune with her voice by going into the Alabaster Tower. If anyone is cursed with the Ingrate's Retribution and seeks to atone, they will have to come here and call forth their witnesses (Arkadi Orkani will allow all the creatures of Arkadia to witness to the cursed's willingness to obey the laws of Arkadia or his/her obstinacy in defying them, even after they were cursed).

At the bottom of the spiral staircase...

About 100 feet down (and that's a lot of dizzying turns for anyone using that staircase), there is a huge open cubic chamber that appears to be another 100 feet on every side. The staircase is about 50 feet off-center. All around the staircase and leading up to the hewn stone walls is a wooden floor that consists of two colors of wood panels that, even from above, don't seem to be laid out in any recognizable pattern.

At the center of all this is a 30-foot high pyramid-like structure of small boulders stacked on top of each other. Each boulder is about one foot in diameter. Past that on the far wall is a huge and ornate door at least 50 feet wide and 25 feet tall. There is a caption inscribed in each of the five Ancient Race languages, but you are too far away to see what it might say, and besides, the rocky pyramid is blocking some of your view.

The caption is chiseled into the stone above the huge wooden doors and reads: "Final Resting Place" in Ancient Arkadian on top, with, following in order beneath, Ancient Astorian, Ancient Ammorian, Ancient Oshekogan, and Ancient Atlantean (as opposed to the modern version of those races; think Old English vs. modern-day English: very much a different language with some similarities.

The floor is only a puzzle if it is vocalized by the players as maybe being a puzzle. If none of them vocalize it (by cautioning another of the party from stepping on one of the wooden panels without first figuring out if there are traps, for instance) then it is not a puzzle (to the pure all things are pure).

If the floor becomes a puzzle, that means they are unfamiliar with this place, and intruders who must now pass a test in order to walk around freely in this chamber.

Here's the puzzle: have them roll their TAC while you secretly roll their WIL (which represents the strength of their conviction). If you win the OPPROLL (meaning WIL was higher), then the wooden panel was a trap and it simply falls open like a trap door, letting whatever/whoever (if they failed their REFLEX Common Ability roll) was on that HEX drop to the darkness below (and this can go wherever you decide: Faerie Realm (then they have to get out of Faerie Realm to complete the Adventure), spikes, water, fire, the DreamScape...use your imagination, Storyteller!

If they win the OPPROLL, then their Technical Acuity (TAC) has convinced their conviction (WIL) that there's a trap *that the floor panel is solid and not part of the trap.*

Your players will probably hate you for this puzzle, but hey, it was of their own doing!

REASON FOR THIS PUZZLE: A lesson in Glimmering. The strength of a Glimmering (even the tensile strength) depends on the person's belief that the Glimmering is real. There is, in fact, NO floor in this huge chamber, which simply keeps dropping down endlessly. The entire floor is a Greater Glimmering B=100g. And you (Storyteller)...uh we mean Arkadi Orkani... can make the Floor and what's beneath anything you want... because it's a Glimmering!

If the players defiantly keep descending (after discovering it's all a Glimmering and somehow seeing past it's huge Potency (any CRIT will do)), then the deep shaft will eventually turn and reveal a giant (1000 foot long/high) chained Cerberus (STATLINE 5:1... monster) restricting access to the chamber behind it which glows with emerald green light. (This is the Emerald Tower spoken of in *The Starborn War* (Book 2 of the Immortal Empires series) and it is not a Glimmering).

THE ROCK PYRAMID

While not initially aroused, even if they are touched, the boulders (who are really Rock-men, Fey that somehow escaped the Cast of Woes), act like normal boulders. BUT, if removed from their place, they will simply "roll" or "walk" back up to where they were, hopefully when no one is looking.

If they are removed from their place a second time, the Rockmen will attack, revealing a solitary, but dead, white birch tree at the center of their pyramid. You'll need to use the Overbearing Rules (SC177) for a proper handling of this encounter.

There are 30 rockmen (and the rest are indeed normal boulders):

Rockman 2:5/090/000/1-1:1040exp

Rockmen only speak one word at a time and can only say verbs ("will attack" is two words, so that wouldn't work even though it is one verb). The ONLY other word they can say is "NO." They never say "Yes." An example would be: "Attack!" while another few rockmen answer "Attacking!" while one of them who has attacked says "Attacked!"

Though their speech is limited, Rockmen are quite crafty and know how to Overbear their opponents. They are so small that eight of them can attack one 7-foot tall Ancient Race adult at a time (conduct your Overbearing attacks accordingly).

If the party can convince them that they are here to revive the White Birch (that they are protecting) and not hurt it, the rockmen will stop attacking. Otherwise, the rockmen will chase them away from the tree until they go back up the spiral staircase (the rockmen cannot fly, nor will they venture further away from the tree than the staircase). They will then re-form around the White Birch tree to continue protecting her...

THE WHITE BIRCH - SPIRIT (PART 3)

Though at first appearing completely dead with its bark rolling away from it like paper, the White Birch has one solitary silver leaf holding on to dear life on one of the branches. Funny how you did not notice it before.

Perhaps it could be said that the players' hope that this "last" tree isn't completely dead is what manifested the leaf...

The White Birch tree is actually Boreas (Lady Spirit), who was Shapeshifted into the White Birch by Antara and then suspended in mid-air so as to die (which, of course, has already happened, as her roots could not find any soil or water). The last leaf is actually a manifestation of the Original Element: Elemental Spirit.

As used in the Game, Elemental (magical) Spirit has nothing to do with intelligent "spirits" (Restless Shamed/Unashamed). Instead, Elemental Spirit is a "feeling" or deep "emotion" that takes over an intelligent being, and therefore has Potency and can be resisted by MResist.

Counter-intuitively, the only way to save the tree is to pluck the last leaf from its branches. Whoever plucks the last leaf is hopefully the character that will play (or be the Bonded Warrior to) Boreas. If not, then that person will be overcome with a strong desire to "touch" the character that is Boreas reincarnated (or who is her Bonded Warrior if they haven't found Boreas yet if you're playing the variation of this game...then the Bonded Warrior-to-be will transfer the Original Element over to Boreas during their re-bonding ritual).

THE FINAL RESTING PLACE

If the players have the remains of any of the prior reincarnations of the Original Coven, they can freely pass through the great wooden door into this dimly-lit (with luminescent moss and fireflies that seem to be nested in the moss) large (but smaller) chamber that houses 25 mausoleums (5 for each of the coven members; one for each of their reincarnations Antara promised).

The party can lay them to rest (in the 4th Mausoleum, each, preferably, which bears witness to the dire fact that there is but ONE chance left (as the party IS the LAST reincarnation) to open the Cave of Dreams and free the fey!

Hopefully, this will bring a sober realization to the players that these Original Coven members must now be protected at all costs, and they must definitely NOT take unwarranted risks.

THE MANIFESTATION

Once the players have recovered all of the Original Elements (and assuming you're not playing the variation of this Adventure), you can make them transform into the Original Coven (give them copies of the Character Records in the Appendix). They will suddenly "remember" all the skills on those Character Records and also how to use the Original Elements (and how to behave as a Coven).

As manifested, they will be a Lesser Coven, meaning that in order to cast magic with Greater Effect (Potency = g) they will all have to be touching each other, and cast through Boreas only (Greater Covens need not touch each other -- only be within their MAF x Hexes of each other). It's up to you if you want to make them a Greater Coven, say, with some reward/blessing from Arkadi Orkani (or Queen Brûd) for saving the lives of the young Arkadian Kraal Warriors or saving Jentha from the Black Forest; *but keep in mind that a Greater Coven is also when each coven member has at least a Rank 1 in Greater Magic in their own Element: in this way they would be able to cast Greater Magic by themselves (in their own element) without the need to come together as a Coven (which they would do to increase Potency or to cast a spell that is not their element)).*

The Original Coven members have the following attributes:

- The Original Elements simply swim around and in and out of the coven member's body/eyes/nose/ears without any harm to them. Other benefits include:
- Can cast magic with their own Element without any source present (the Original Element IS the source);
- Completely immune to mundane and magical harm that might have been caused by their own element type. (Malekbel cannot be harmed by nonmagical or magical fire; Karfyn cannot drown in water, Arumbrek cannot be suffocated in earth; Boreas cannot succumb to emotions (Elemental Spirits or Charms that attempt to change her emotions); Achernar cannot be pummeled by or otherwise damaged by air/tornadoes; etc.;
- All magical casts with their unique element using their Original Element as the source adds +2/die Potency; if casting Greater Magic through Boreas, they gain +10/die (and can opt for Greater Effect (Potency/Binding is Greater Magic).

Make a big deal out of their transformation! It is a significant accomplishment in this Adventure, well-earned!

LEVEL of Players' Characters Now

We're expecting that the players by now are ORank=5, between personal experience rewards, group experience awards, and Bonus awards for completing sections (in which you can award the whole group 20,000 experience points, say). Remember, these experience point awards are then divided by their Fortune Point Ratio to see how many FPs they have available to use

for buying up their skills to satisfy the Skill Prerequisites tables on AR56. While you can do it any way you see fit, our intent in this Adventure is for the characters (with stats) the players were playing to become the status for the Coven's bonded warriors, as the Original Coven members in the Appendix are already pre-made and all of them are ORank=7.

Particularly skilled players will be able to manage with an ORank=4 Bonded Warrior, But we're assuming ORank=5 and up for the Adventure difficulty that awaits. Here's a summary just to help you plan your awards up until now:

- **Per character:**
- ORank=0 to 1: **230 FPs**
- ORank=1 to 2: **670 FPs**
- ORank=2 to 3: **1200 FPs**
- ORank=3 to 4: **2020 FPs**
- ORank=4 to 5: **2760 FPs**

for a Total of 6,880 total FPs spent on bringing skills up. Just that minimum would put them at Glory=4L, and to be ORank=5 they would need a minimum of 175,000 Experience Points. At a FP Ratio of 25:1, 175,000 Experience Points yields exactly 7000 FPs, so that should not be a problem.

That said, you should be aware that if you have a Master Scholar among your players (with a FP Ratio of 100:1), they'll need 4 times as many experience points just to get the same amount of Fortune Points as the 25:1 character. If this is the case, then you must throw additional challenges at the party in order to bring everyone up to the Rank they need to be.

Lastly, an ORank=5 also yields 5+4+3+2+1 ORanks of X-Pts (15 X-Pts) which the players can use to increase their Main Attributes (and get other permanent bonuses). See AR60 on what they can spend their X-Pts on.

One word of advice: It would behoove a couple of them to ensure their MAF is high in order to cast higher Potency spells (for Lesser Magic, the number of Potency dice is limited to MAF+MYS Rank (AR127)). Not all "Bonded Warrior" work will be swinging swords, and this will give them some extra firepower when the Coven might be unable to cast.

Projected Experience Awards By Section

- **Act 1:** 25,000 (role-playing, fights, info-gathering)
- **Act 2:** 50k to 75k (encounters along the journey)
- **Intermission:** 20k-25k per Test + Manifestation Award

If you plan each of these sections with enough extra encounters/traps/tests/side missions to reach these experience point milestones, you'll accomplish two things: [1] you'll get the characters to where they need to be to serve as effective Bonded Warriors; [2] you'll make this Adventure a unique experience unlike any other Storyteller's version of this Cave of Dreams Adventure. Run with it! By the way, the Manifestation Award can be the "cheesing it" award just to bring them all up to ORank=5.

Act 3: The Cave of Dreams

Preliminaries

By this point, we are moving forward with the following assumptions:

[1] The Original Coven has been found and is reunited;

[2] The Original Coven enjoys the protection of 5 Bonded Warriors, with each Bonded Warrior assigned to and sharing a special bond with a particular coven member;

[3] The type of Bond each Bonded Warrior enjoys with their coven member is the Arkadian Bond *Kiss of the Faerie Queen* (AR178-9); alternatively (if you think that is too strong a bond for the way you Storytell), you can choose the Arvalis's *Warrior's Bond* (AR181).

[4] Your massive "end of Intermission" Admin Session is completed, everyone is leveled up, everyone is familiar with their new Coven Member characters' abilities, time was allotted for the making/acquiring of MenH-g weapons and/or helpful items for defense and survival.

[5] A Marune Minion has evaded their capture and will attack them when an opportunity presents itself (in an attempt to foil their plans to open the Cave of Dreams).

The Fellowship of the Cave Ceremony

When you've got everyone ready, you'll do well to have a little party for them with all the big shots. The unexplained absence of a couple of the big shots they expected to be there will be revealed later.

Ceremony Attendees - the Hidden Vale, Arkadia

Arkadian True Archon Simcha and a group of subservient Vale Warriors, Master Scholar Ophelia Hadriana and her father Octavian Hadrian, Aunt Julia, Legate Maximillian Rufus and his Primus Pilus Adolfo Mactator, Albanaeus Rufus, Bernardin Atilius with his Arkadian animal pet "Wolf."

All attendees will be very deferential to the Original Coven, treating them with the utmost respect, and deigning to give them gifts they hope will help them on their journey to the Cave of Dreams.

Maximillian will give apologies that Empress Maximina had business and could not attend, but will get into an argument with Albanaeus over the latter's assertion that she is a Marune. After a while, Simcha will shut them both up with a slap across the louder one's face and a glare of warning to the other.

Ophelia will be able to give them a Greater Magic defense each of what is requested of her (each Coven Member should have their own request). And as for the Bonded Warriors, she will give them Lesser Magic protections (as she expects one of them to be sacrificed in order for the coven to be able to enter the Cave of Dreams, and she does not want to waste her precious Greater magic on them).

Simcha (or Aunt Julia if you've opted for the Arvalis Warrior Bonds) will bestow the magical bonds upon the Bonded Warriors and tie them to a specific coven member.

Octavian Hadrian and Adolfo have brought all manner of weapons and armor to outfit the bonded warriors with some MenH-L/g stuff.

Albanaeus will tell them all about what to expect on entering the dead badlands of Wyrmkyn Kyngdom, including how the Wyrmkyn use Blood Magic.

Maximillian, when he isn't arguing with Albanaeus or being distracted by Simcha's smooth thighs and long hair, will give advice on the proper military role a bonded warrior must play, and how they can work together to protect the coven so that the coven is free to cast spells without being interrupted by attackers.

When everyone has had their fill of food and drink and discussion, and the players feel like they are prepared, it's time for them to go.

With Simcha's permission, Ophelia Travels the entire 10-member group to just west of the Wyrmkyn Kyngdom: the Ural Mountains in the heart of the dangerous Scythian barbarian lands north of the Caspian Sea.

(The players will have to roll the MResist for this Travel spell and any other protective spells Ophelia placed on anyone). She will get upset and snippety if any of her spells are resisted against where she has to cast them again.

The Chase

Probably on purpose, Ophelia Travels the group of five Original Coven members and their five Bonded Warriors to a place she knows is currently being overrun by a Scythian barbarian horde: a small Celt village that the Astorian Frumentarii have secretly supported in order to keep eyes and ears on who was using this passage to enter and exit Wyrmkyn Kyngdom.

Ophelia knows that the Barbarian Horde cannot possibly withstand the power of the Original Coven, especially if they cast a Greater Magic Offensive spell against them. So, in her mind, their victory over the 500 invaders will give them a confidence booster. Nevertheless, Ophelia will also Travel there, but invisibly, just to ensure (if needed) the Original Coven's survival.

It's up to you whether she will actually "watch over" them in Wyrmkyn Kyngdom. But odds are that her love for Optimus Verus will drive her on ahead of them to enter the Cave of Dreams and try to save him (for she knows that he went there and has not yet returned). Thus, if you take this recommended option, make sure to note that there is fresh blood (only a couple of days old, say) on the stone slab that demands a blood sacrifice to open the Cave of Dreams entrance.

After the part arrives in Sealladh (which means "Overlook" in Scots Gaelic, or for our purposes, Starborn Celtic), read to them the following:

Once again, in the blink of an eye, the scenery has changed. This time, from the lush paradisaical garden of Arkadia to a dusty and dry outpost on the barren foothills of the badlands of Wyrmkyn Kyngdom. It is night, but there is a full moon and fire everywhere in the village. Harrowing screams and maniacal laughter of frenzied warriors from all around pierce your ears. Half-naked barbarians are taking great delight in slaughtering the tattooed Celtic populace of this village. As there are women and children still fleeing, it looks like the attack has just begun; indeed, the barbarians, Scythian by their markings (a Newborn race), are still throwing torches onto the dry rooftops of the village huts. While the Starborn Celts are more magical than the Newborn invaders, they have just been overwhelmed by the sheer numbers, well into the several hundred, of attackers. It takes only seconds for you to take all of this in, and just as long for dozens of the attacking horde to notice that a new enemy has arrived right in the center of the village. Rather than cower for fear, the wolf-headed and axe wielding men rush at you from all sides shouting their war cries.

REACTION.

Barbarian Miles (500): 2:2/222/222/222:1000exp

Barbarian Centurion (5): 2:7/777/777/775:1960exp

Barbarian Legate (1): 2:9/999/999/995:2860exp

*We use the Fey Statline Chart in the SC103 for convenience, even though these barbarians are certainly not fey. Therefore, any MTAP or Magical effects you allow them to have will most certainly be in the form of MenH items, as Newborn are the least magical of all the race categories.

**Also, remember to use the Experience Point Awards Guideline (SC175), especially as pertains to the % Abilities Used against Players. Although the Coven may win the Reaction and instantly wipe out all the Barbarians with one MG Fire spell, that would only be a Great/Superior idea and no experience would be awarded (i.e. 500 miles soldiers x 1000 exp) for killing them because 0% of the miles' abilities were used against the party.

***When figuring MResist on a mass scale like this, remember that odds are 100:1 to roll a CRIT resistance (double 10s on the Gold Dice). So you can safely assume that at least one miles from every century CRIT resisted the Coven's spell (for a total of 5 Survivors, not including the Centurions or Legate).

Try to give the Coven a good fight, with the Centurions being sneaky, using arrows, hiding from sight, etc. Even the Legate might have a couple magical protections (against fire even, because he knew they were going to burn the place) from their Blood Shaman Marune Minion leader (who is watching all of this from afar). After your Marune Minion sees how powerful the Coven is, s/he might just wait to attack them in Wyrmkyn Kyngdom where their magic will not work rather than attack them now.

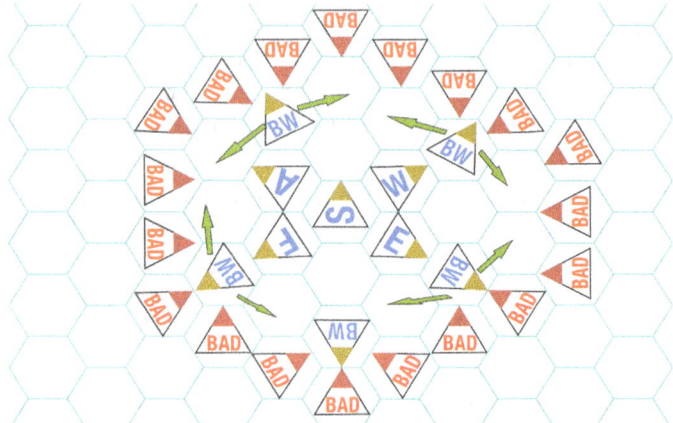

On a hex map, the Bonded Warriors might have to defend against 3-4 attacks in the same Phase as they are bumrushed by the Barbarians (assuming the Coven is in the middle and attempting to cast rather than individually fight such a massive horde. During the cast, all but Spirit (who is actually the one casting) can use one hand to defend themselves (as the other is touching either Spirit or another Coven Member. But Spirit must remain free from distraction for her cast to be successful.

{**The advantages a Greater Coven now become self-evident in not having to touch each other: mobility, the ability to not only defend but also to attack, while Spirit does her thing.** *Remember: while Spirit is casting <u>as a Coven</u>, no other Coven Members can cast* (this goes for Greater Covens as well).}

If the Coven decides to levitate or fly up from the attacking horde, the Blood Shaman Marune Minion will expose him/herself by casting Blood Magic to make several dozen of the horde soldiers also fly; however, they will not be used to this and all of them will receive the [P]enalty die to their attacks. Keep in mind that airborne combatants have two extra attack hexes (as well as hexes they must defend against): above and below, so it might just be a better idea to stay on the ground!

If/when the Blood Shaman sees that the Coven easily did away with the Barbarian Horde, s/he will use Blood Magic to raise up the horde and make them immune to the type of attack (presumably fire) that the Coven used to kill them the first time. But doing this will expose the Blood Shaman as the source of the Blood Magic spell (the eerie bright red blood swirling about him/her and all the plants and small animals dying around him/her will be a dead give-away. If discovered, the Blood Shaman now wears his/her Rainbow Marune Eyes openly, when discovered. S/he is taking a stand to kill the coven right here, right now. The Blood Shaman will have prepared for the fight with several Defenses, Protections, and ensuring that their Marune Gifts are ready...so have fun!

If the Coven chooses to flee rather than show its might, the Barbarians will chase them to the border of Wyrmkyn Kyngdom, but go no further. The Marune Minion, however, being as yet undiscovered, will follow them in and wait for an opportunity to kill them all, even perhaps, using a Marune Gift or two to force a couple Wyrmkyn warriors to do his bidding.

Only the Barbarian Centurions and Legate will have any loot of value to the party. Prepare appropriately.

WYRMKYN KYNGDOM

The first thing that lets you know you've crossed over the boundary into Wyrmkyn Kyngdom is the stench in the air. It's like the bad breath of someone suffering from halitosis, all that decaying blood in their gums. It's a mystery to you, since all around you is barren wilderness with skaggy mountainous cliffs pointing defiantly up into the sky. Rock and sand. No vegetation to look at. No animals running from you. Just you and...and death, so it would seem. Your knowledge that creatures called Wyrmkyn live in these regions is not comforting. If they can survive in so barren a landscape, they must be tougher than your own breast-fed pampered upbringing has made you.

As you venture further in, you get to feeling sick to your stomach, but it isn't because of the blood stench. Although it's only happened maybe once before to you, you're quite aware that your access to the Weave attenuates with every advancing step. Any further, and you'll not be able to cast any spells at all. Hopefully, you didn't use all your anchored spells yet.

Now's the time they can turn back if they really were not prepared to enter Wyrmkyn Kyngdom and be cut off from the Weave. However, depending on how they handled the Horde, they might not be able to, since the Horde will certainly be waiting for them for a while.

How long they spend winding up and down the mountains to find the blood altar is up to you, but we suggest that before they make it to the entrance (the Cave of Dreams Altar), they:

[1] defeated the Blood Shaman Marune Minion;

[2] defeated or fled from a group of low-level Wyrmkyn shapeshifters;

[3] defeated the Wyrmkyn Mantis who "guards" the entrance in order to extort those who want to enter. He will demand their most precious MenH items from them and one of their number to take as a slave (and he most certainly will choose the pretty Spirit coven member). Some good role playing should come out of this. Depending on the strength of the Party, perhaps the Wyrmkyn Mantis will have a "wife" who helps him extort petition-

ers seeking entrance to the Cave. No amount of explaining will convince the Wyrmkyn to help the party in the slightest. And as Wyrmkyn are resistant to Charm magic and have a high degree of resistance to Elemental:Spirit because of their permanent Corrupted Mens (51% Corrupted), the party can either give away their precious items or fight to the death (which might be good anyway, since the altar needs a blood sacrifice...).

LOW LEVEL WYRMKYN WARRIORS				
PHQ	5	TAC	0	MResist: 2d10g +	3d10+10
PHL	3	SOC	1	PResist: 2d10g +	2d10+15
AGL	3	CBT	2	Awareness:: 2d10g +	0
COR	3	END	2	MTAP:	475
INT	2	ART	1	SK:Casting	R1
INS	1	MYS	2	SK:Short Blades	R3
WIL	3	BV	240	SK:Dodge	R4
EMP	0	DV	5/15	Other Primary Skills:	R2
MAF	5	MVT	5	Synergy	203
100% EXP:	7000			MCTRL:	71 (Curative only)

ORank = 5 (Blood Vale Warrior use AR72) +15 LUCK (one roll per day), PHQ yields +10 damage; Talents: CBT5:Bantam's Benefit, Clusyth's Barbican; CBT0:Dodge Distancer; AGL5:Hands are Quicker; COR5:Balance Beam Acrobatics; COR10:Lightning Reflexes, Surefoot; AGL10:Sticky Feet; AGL25:Klyrath's Agility; CBT25:Carnage Ferocity

True Spells:: See Appendix	Blood Letting, Incision
MenH Items: Stone Sword	B=25L +2w Primary/+2T2 Secondary
Breach-clout	B=30L +1d10 MResist, +10 DV Total Body

WYRMKYN MANTIS OF TOPHYT GUARDIAN				
PHQ	7	TAC	2	MResist: 2d10g +	3d10+14
PHL	7	SOC	2	PResist: 2d10g +	4d10+14
AGL	7	CBT	4	Awareness: 2d10g +	2d10
COR	7	END	3	MTAP:	700
INT	5	ART	3	SK:Casting	R4
INS	3	MYS	3	SK:Long Blades	R5 + [M]
WIL	5	BV	260	SK:Dodge	R5 + [M]
EMP	2	DV	20	Other Primary Skills:	R4
MAF	7	MVT	7	Synergy	330
100% EXP:	28,000			MCTRL:	40m/81S/121M

ORank=7 (R3 Arkadian Animal Forms Corrupted Guardian, R4 Mantis of Tophyt (SC74)); +14 LUCK (one roll per day); PHQ yields +14 damage; FA Powers: Nature's Harmony, The Prayer, The Demand, Scourge of Nature, Wrath of the Wyrmkyn plus 7xPhysical, 2xIntellectual, 1xSpiritual, and 2xArcane you choose; Flow of War 5; you choose the Talents (as R7 Guardian).

True Spells:: See Appendix	Incision-Forced Bloodlettg, Blood Elemental
MenH Items: Black Gold Ring	B=5g +[M] die to Long Blades & Dodge, ring is Conjuring Relic: Cimmeria
Magical Access: M: CON/CUR/OFF, S: ALT, BEN, m:TIM, none to the rest.	

Admittedly, the Mantis of Tophyt is a badass! Hopefully, each member of the Coven survives, even, if need be, at the expense of the lives of the Bonded Warriors, who should have done everything, even to the sacrifice of themselves to ensure the Coven members victory. If ANY of the Coven members is killed, you can either say they failed at this point (as obviously the Coven Member killed was not the REAL Original Coven member...), or *not let them know and just let them continue on (recommended).*

If one or more of the Coven is killed, the Original Elements will be able to be taken off their bodies, but will not respond at all magically to another who is not a Coven member of the same type (fire, water, etc.). That means that the Coven's days of Casting Greater Magic as a Coven are over. The survivors, however, will still be able to cast their own elemental magic with their Original Elements.

If not forcibly taken off the dead coven member, the Original Element will still float around and in and out of the body of its coven member. The survivors are free to take the corpse(s) with them into the Cave of Dreams, but the corpses will not be able to voluntarily sit the Thrones, obviously. At least 5 survivors are needed to complete the quest; if fewer than 5 have survived to this point, we recommend you let them continue on and then ultimately fail in the Throne Room, where perhaps someone will be able to find their way out to convince Maximillian to try another attempt at finding the true Coven.

This narrative assumes all five of the Original Coven members have survived; you'll have to change it to fit your own situation if not.

THE CAVE OF DREAMS ALTAR

Climbing up the jagged path you discovered was not easy as the path certainly seemed to disappear several times. You nearly lost your balance more than once, and were it not for shear luck you may have been impaled on the pointy crags hundreds of feet below.

There were no eagles nests, no snakes, nothing living to obstruct your ascent, except for that vicious Wyrmkyn shapeshifter, of course. Hopefully, you'll find another way out of this wicked land, assuming you'll make it out. Were it not for the tenuous promise of the psychotic Antara, and your belief that you're the chosen ones, the true reincarnations of the Original Coven, there is no doubt you'd be hastening straight to your own eternal imprisonment in the Cave of Dreams.

A wave of doubt suddenly crosses your heart as you reach what is a small plateau with a rather large altar-looking slab laid horizontally on six short columns of stone. On the far side of the plateau rises another crag about forty more feet into the sky, a sharp point its zenith, and the face of that cliff is sheer, like glass. But it is opaque, reflecting only the altar and yourselves as in a darkened mirror.

A glimpse? Did you see that? Perhaps it was a figment of your imagination, perhaps your fears playing on you, but you could've sworn that your reflection only fifty feet away suddenly cut the throat of your neighbor. But looking again, there is only your reflection, obediently mirroring your every movement.

A breeze carries the unmistakable odor of blood your way. On top of the altar-slab, blood bright red, and recently given, fills each etching to the brim, making it clearly easy to read. Carved into the stone slab in large letters, and in each of the five Ancient Languages is an inscription that reads: "Only by Blood Sacrifice Shalt Thou Enter."

The Environment Here

As the players ascended the path, you should have randomly rolled to see which of them would have to roll their reflexes or fall and take damage and have to climb up again. If they were able to fly up, great, but the plateau itself is a Dead Magic Zone of Rating 4 (DMZ4), which means that no lesser or greater magic works here. This means, they will have their flight magic canceled as soon as they try to hover over the smallest inch of the plateau (the path below can be 10-50 hexes down (roll 1d5) for up to 150+2d10 BV damage at 50 hexes (divided appropriately per body part 10% each arm, 15% each leg, and the rest on Vitals). See AR117. Players will be able to benefit from Magical DV and the Earth Original Coven Member won't be hurt at all by the impact with the rocks below.

> 10 Hexes: 60 + 1d10 falling damage
> 20 Hexes: 80 + 1d10 falling damage
> 30 Hexes: 100 + 1d10 falling damage
> 40 Hexes: 120 + 2d10 falling damage
> 50 Hexes: 130 + 2d10 falling damage

Remember that there is no Weave with which to cast spells in Wyrmkyn Kyngdom, but already cast spells (anchored spells) can be triggered (so hopefully someone has flight, levitate, or healing as an anchored spell). To clarify, while Wyrmkyn Kyngdom is cut off from the Weave, it is not a Dead Magic Zone that actively cancels magic on it. DMZs are in it (as on this plateau), but they are not Kyngdom-wide.

The DMZ4 on this plateau cancels all Lesser Magic, Greater Magic, and MenH-L items, and dampens Greater Magic items (suppresses them so that they cannot function until they are out of the DMZ). Furthermore, only Fighting Art powers of RTG4 or higher work here (see AR173).

The altar and the glassy crag are indestructible, as is the entire mountain (not even F5 Greater earth elementals can alter it in any way). It is held together with the huge blood magic Greater Coven Cast of Woes in the First Age.

Role-Playing

The "wave of doubt" that rolls over the party is indeed a Greater Magic Elemental Spirit effect, and the only one who is immune to it is Lady Spirit (Boreas). Boreas will have to get everyone together to cast a Utility:Destroy Binding (with Greater Effect) spell for those who did not resist it: ELEM SPIRIT(Doubt):POT=50g, Duration: 1d10 Minutes.

Those who are effected by the Doubt have second thoughts about anything to do with the Cave of Dreams and start climbing back down the mountain after a short role-play of trying to convince the rest of the party to abandon the quest as well.

A Quick Reminder on Resisting Greater Magic

A player's character that is of Greater Glory resists both ML and MG point for point. If a character is not yet of Greater Glory, the Greater Magic POTency is multiplied by 5 before the MResist Roll (see SC63:"Resisting Greater Magic").

For example, say Malekbel and his Bonded Warrior both roll 40 MResist against the MG:Doubt of POT=50g. Malekbel has achieved Glory 2 Greater and his Bonded Warrior is at Glory 5 Lesser (your Adventure may be different). Malekbel would then succumb to the Doubt magic, which would have a Binding = 10g on him, and his Bonded Warrior would also succumb but with Binding = 50g x 5 = 250 minus MResist of 40 = 210g.

A Lesser Magic Destroy Binding (after it gets through MResist) of B=210L with Days duration would be able to "Dampen" the B=210g (Greater) effect for as many Phases as they rolled days duration, but only a Greater Magic cast will be able to actually Destroy the MG Binding. A Greater Magic Destroy Binding spell that gets, say, 1 point through MResist for a B=1g would completely Destroy the B=210g in 210 Phases, so long as the Destroy Binding Duration was at least that long (AR153). It will be nigh impossible for any of the party to cast with such high Potency, but they can cast several smaller Destroy Binding spells, even with Lesser Magic, or use other methods, to get the Coven to touch so that Spirit can cast a Destroy Binding with Greater effect and save everyone's ass.

You might object that achieving Greater Glory thus drastically reduces Greater Magic efficacy, bringing it down to the ML level. But, you would be forgetting the Expanded capabilities of Greater Magic and the fact that one affected by it would also have to have Greater Magic access just to Destroy Binding on whatever s/he didn't resist (in that a B=1g OFFENSIVE Binding would effectively kill an Ancient Race character of BV=200 in 200 Phases (a little over 13 minutes), were s/he not able to Destroy the binding.). So, Greater Magic is STILL a formidable weapon against those of Greater Glory.

What will probably prove a great relief to the players is the fact that no blood magic can be cast on the Plateau and it is also canceled, so if they were suffering from any Blood Magic binding, it will be completely Destroyed once they reach the Plateau. The Mens Corruption that may have resulted does not "heal," however, and they will have to role-play accordingly.

Because of the Doubt and potential Mens Corruption, as well as the inevitable discussion about how/who they are going to sacrifice on the altar, there should be ample role-playing here. Hopefully, you'll be able to sit back and listen to your players talk through things.

While the party might be of the opinion that a full blood-death sacrifice (killing) must be made, that is not the case. The glassy face will become nearly transparent to any who spills his/her own blood on the altar, as long as it is enough to fill one etched letter. A full sacrifice (killing of a Ancient Race/Starborn/Newborn and letting them bleed out on the Altar) opens the Cave of Dreams entrance for all who were on the Plateau at the time of the killing. Animal sacrifices do not open the Cave of Dreams (unless the animal is a paragon like Jentha, the first horse), because their blood is just not powerful enough.

The Cave of Dreams entrance is all mechanic; there is no Power or any type of deity, and so "Altar" might be a misnomer, one that the Mantis of Tophyt might try to exploit in an attempt to cause the party to fear him/her in the attempt to extort them.

Inside the Cave of Dreams

Stepping through the nearly transparent "glass" is like walking through air: there was absolutely no resistance whatsoever. It's like the Cave wants you to enter, having tasted of what you have to offer. Behind you, you see yourself being sacrificed on the altar. You know it's just a hallucination, you hope. The Cave is trying to scare you. You hear whispers and accusations all around you. Voices assert that you're a selfish bastard. They claim you should have sacrificed yourself but you were just a little coward instead. The voices swirl around you, but they could be in your head. The other members of your party seem to hear stuff too. But are they hearing what you are?

It's dark inside the Cave. The only source of light is the light through the still as yet transparent glassy entrance, and once that becomes opaque again, it will be dark. The light from Fire's Original Element will simply not be enough to light the way, and the floor seems slippery. It's cold in here. There's no smell. You know once that glassy wall turns back to rock, there'll be no going back.

Allow one final second for any player to change their mind about entering and then shut them in! The only way now is deeper into the Cave of Dreams!

Until they get to the first chamber, the way is dark and narrow, and there appear to be huge bottomless drop-offs on either side of the path (in fact, it might be wise to crawl, just to make sure you don't step/slip off the path to the fathoms below).

While in the Cave of Dreams...

The Cave of Dreams is fraught with dangers and indestructible terrors. It is a unique place (actually a Pocket Dimension) with its own laws of physics, magic, and so on. You're free to add your own, but here's what they should be at a minimum:

1. Magic cannot effect the Cave of Dreams at all, not even Alteration Magic on its walls, floors, etc., *unless otherwise specifically allowed.* Travel Magic does not work in the Cave of Dreams.

2. Physical attacks of any type do not harm the Cave of Dreams in any way, as the whole structure is made of Blood-Magicked Dream Essence. Thus, even some DreamCarvers have met their

own fate thinking they could manipulate the Cave of Dreams to their own wills. The Cave might respond to a DreamCarver's powers, but in unexpected — and deadly — ways.

3. The Cave of Dreams labyrinth can be as convoluted as you wish, with gravity (or none) anywhere pointing "down" in any direction you wish. Each chamber is yet another dire test. Every hallway (after the first from the entrance) is illuminated by an eerie light blue glow coming from the ice-appearing walls that extend so high "up" from the floor that one cannot see the ceiling (it just looks like the walls meet, but one cannot tell how high up they meet).

4. The tests going to the Throne chamber usually try to turn one member of a group against the other, try to destroy teamwork and create distrust among party members. The tests for a freed Throne sitter leading out of the Throne chamber and out of the Cave are more individual and tempt personal ambition, vengeance desires, greed, lust, power, etc. (It is important to note that there are no paths leading out of the Cave of Dreams until it is "opened" by the Coven). Only ex-Throne sitters passing these tests and finding a portal back to their worlds achieve their Immortal Event; those who escape the Cave, even having sat a throne, by other (quicker/safer) means do not gain that benefit.

5. Eventually, after surviving several tests on their way to the Throne Room, the party will arrive there. You decide how many tests your party must undergo before that happens (as there is no "shortest route" to get there); it is solely dependent on the tests.

6. The Cave of Dreams exists in several worlds and in the Dream-Scape simultaneously.

7. The whole Cave is cold (about 50 degrees F), and the icy walls are really not freezing cold (but touching the icy walls might be deadly! (see Hall of Regret, below).

8. The walls of the Cave of Dreams produce CRIT:1 Hallucinations (of your whim and they need a MResist of CRIT:1 or better to see them for what they are). Outside the powerful hallucination, the walls have hands or tentacles that grow towards the victim the more s/he participates (does not resist) the hallucination's temptation(s). The hallucination fades once they are trapped behind the ice. Typically, there is something "wrong" with the hallucination that gives the victim a chance to shake it off.

GRAND HALL OF REGRET (TEMPTATION)

The darkness of the entry path gives way to an eerie blue illumination that glows off the walls of ice to either side of the path in front of you. While it feels good to finally have walls that should prevent anyone from falling to their deaths if they slip off the path, the walls themselves do not seem friendly at all.

Trapped within the ice, just inches into the walls on either side are all manner of races, of vocations of people, like yourselves, who have dared enter this dreadful place. Behind them, and deeper into what might be an endless "wall" of ice, you can make out hundreds of others that were trapped before them, until finally the clear ice gets so thick as to become opaque. Some have their backs to you, others their faces. The ones whose faces you can see are caught in a constant state of horror as they realized, during their last moments,

that their death was imminent. Many of them have blood frozen at the ends of their fingers where they tried to claw their way out through the ice. A few others merely reflect the sadness they felt when they realized their fate. There's no sign, however, on how they got into the ice.

Further down the hall, about one hundred feet, the path winds to the right, and to get to that bend, you'll have to traverse this corridor of death, of countless trapped adventurers who failed to make it out of this place alive.

Wait, did you hear that? Was it in your head or out? But it was definitely a voice, a whisper, did it come from that Arkadian staring at you in with horror-filled eyes, looking at you wide-eyed through the thin later of ice that keeps him trapped? Is he alive, can you rescue him? Do you want to?

Perhaps not, for after the unintelligible whisper, you clearly heard another one: "Dream. Yes. You'll dream too."

Now allow for the party to react. If they try to help the Arkadian in any way, the Arkadian suddenly reaches through the ice and grabs the closest person to forcibly drag him/her into the ice. The ice closes instantly on whatever is dragged into it, allowing it to sink in further but not out. The Arkadian moves so quickly, he has a 99% Reflexes score. The victim can roll his/her Reflexes as well, and the larger DTN (differential target number) result wins. [If you roll 45% for the Arkadian, 99-45=54DTN. The victim would have to roll 54% under their own Reflexes in order to avoid getting grabbed.] The Arkadian has two hands, and so will try to grab another victim within reach (1 Hex) if he can after you call REACTION and his turn comes up. His Reaction is 20+5d10. The Arkadian has 300BV and an MResist of 25+4d10. He will not talk, and his mind only "sees" what the Cave wants him to dream. (So if the party somehow reads his mind, you can come up with an elaborate dream as to why the Arkadian decided to grab one or two of them and haul them away!)

Note that only the Arkadian's hands and arms extend out of the ice; he will not come out of the ice. If the victim(s) escape his grasp, he will follow them the whole length of the hallway, weaving in and out of other trapped bodies, with hateful (corrupted?) eyes staring at the party, looking for an opportunity to snatch one of them again.

In order to escape the Arkadian's hold, you'll have to have the player perform an OPPROLL PHQ vs the Arkadian's PHQ=8 (that's 2d10G + 7d10W + 1d10B for the roll, taking the three highest of the Gold/White and then adding the Blue to that; remember that the 10s are open-ended). If the victim fails the first OPPROLL, s/he gets pulled further into the ice, this time half his/her head (with either his/her face in the ice such that s/he cannot talk or breathe or the side/back; roll a 50/50 to find out which if it is not evident by their actions.

Should the party want to cut off the Arkadian's arms, 30 damage achieves that (there is no DV).

THE CHAMBER OF STARS (TEMPTATION)

What seemed like an endless series of twists and turns, ups and downs of the illuminated ice-hallways — indeed, you don't even know which way is up any longer — finally opens up into a rather huge chamber with an open black sky instead of a ceiling. The sky is beautiful with countless stars arranged in various clusters and patterns you've not seen before, so it obviously is not your world's sky. Some of the stars shimmer and then are gone. Others come into being with a small flash. They are all of various colors, not only white, and some of them seem to slowly move after they are born.

Allow a closer inspection with a TAC roll TN30 to view the next description you can read to them:

With the stars, there are other things up there moving, seen only by the light from the stars as they draw near. These things must be huge — or closer — to be so visible, because they seem to be weaving in and out of the stars themselves.

At this point, allow the players to react. The stars are really dreams of everyone in the Cave of Dreams and in their world. The things flying around among the stars are Dream Terrors, monsters that have escaped one dream or another and now roam freely in the DreamScape.

The Chamber itself is actually in the DreamScape Reflected World, and they can "fly" up to the stars (about 1000 feet above them). There is a vast invisible dome on this chamber (think of it as a "skylight" in the roof of a house). The players will be able to get close enough to see individual dreams (and what's happening in them, so be creative!). They'll also be able to see that the flying things are indeed monsters (Dream Terrors) of every sort of abominable thing one can imagine and dream of. They should, at this point, be grateful they are protected by the invisible dome.

However, delaying too long will definitely attract the attention of one or more of the Dream Terrors, who can see the party, too, if they have flown up to the dome. It's up to you if you want the party to fight the Dream Terrors (since they can come INTO the Cave of Dreams Reflected World (which the chamber is), even though they will not be able to go anywhere else but this chamber (not even out through the dome — the Cave of Dreams is closed, remember?).

Dream Terror: 3:9/999/99-/999:10,800exp (no Synergy); can only be affected by MenH-g weapons or magic or DreamCarver abilities. Add 1200 exp per attacking Tentacle you attach (and each extra tentacle at 300BV is 350exp.

and if your Group is powerful enough for a little extra challenge:

Greater Dream Terror: 4:9/999/99-/999:29,250exp plus a couple enhancements from "Other Fey & Monster Enhancements" on SC104.

So, the challenge in this chamber is to make sure the party doesn't get sidetracked. The more they stay and fight (while it's cool to rack up some experience!!!) the more Dream Terrors will

be attracted to the activity. If they're trying to farm the area after the first two Dream Terrors (because maybe they think they're unstoppable), go ahead and throw some R5 paragon-level Dream Terrors in there. At some point, they should realize they're fighting a losing battle and promptly flee out of the chamber, continuing on their journey to the Throne Room. If not, they could all die right here in the DreamScape.

ELEMENTAL WAR CHAMBER (TEMPTATION)

As you approach the next chamber from the twisting path, you notice flickering lights coming from it, howling noises of wind passing your hallway, huge pounding of stone against stone, and crashes of ocean waves against something...big.

Inside this massive chamber which is at least one mile in diameter, there is a massive hill at the center. There are four sections of the room: one that is full of fire elementals battling the center and the sides of their quarter: earth elementals on the one side and air elementals on the side the players are on. The fourth quarter (to the right of where the players are) is filled with water elementals crashing up against the massive hill and the air elementals and earth elementals. The only place where fire and water meet is occasionally in the center when one of them temporarily becomes "King of the Hill" and there is either a water spout on top the hill or a dancing flame (or fire-nado) and massive steam when one kills the other. Otherwise there is a huge humanoid rock elemental on top the hill or a massive air elemental (tornado).

The only element that is not represented is Spirit (and that is actually the hint!).

Remember, the Coven Members are not harmed in any way by their own element. They can venture out into the chamber a little, since Air is on their side, but it's only a matter of time before a tornado comes by and attempts to kill them (the same goes for every other element).

The 100% answer for the whole party to get across is for Spirit to cast (with Greater Effect as a Coven) her Elemental Spirit spell that will "CALM" the elementals within (with as much Potency as she can muster), and then "MARCH" where the Elementals feel the emotion to want to march in circles around the center hill. That way, each coven member can enter into their own element unscathed and "march" along with them until s/he gets to the exit pathway directly across on the other side of the hill (the opening is massive, rising up at least 500 feet, so they can see it over the hill). If there are still Bonded Warriors, they will probably have to opt to walk with Air (Achernar) in the air section around the hill to the exit.

FALSE SHORTCUT (TEMPTATION)

At some point while the party is considering the Elemental War Chamber and how to get across, one of them should notice that the slightly behind where they are standing, the ice wall has opened, showing a short (10 foot-long, 7-foot diameter) tunnel directly into the Throne Room, where they see the Greensteel

Column and Red Crystal Thrones, along with many sleeping fey littering the whole floor. The red crystal thrones seated on the dais in the center of the chamber are empty.

This is not a shortcut, but a trap (two hints: it opens sneakily and silently behind the party and the thrones are empty). This is the "Ice" trying to trick them into it once again. And they will certainly get trapped if they venture down the shortcut. The Cave might even allow them to sit on the fake red crystal thrones before revealing that they are stuck in the ice.

If you want to heighten the suspense, you can let them in but not close the ice immediately, and then discover that the sleeping/dreaming fey littering the floor are all dead! Some frozen, some died from stab wounds, some burned to death (fire), some drowned (water), some got crushed (earth), some got suffocated (air), and some got scared to death (spirit). The last five death descriptions are the harbinger for the Elemental War Chamber, of course, which emphasizes that they should carefully work out a survival plan on how to get to the other side of the War Chamber at some point.

Fortunately, there is a solution for the party if one or more of the Coven members happens to fall to the shortcut temptation (for at this point, the Bonded Warriors really are expendable, but desire may be there to save them so they can keep playing them after the Cave of Dreams Adventure!).

If one Coven Member goes in, all of them need to (they should know by now that the strength of the Coven is them *staying together and within reach of each other!* At some point, whether all of them or a couple of them are in, the ice tunnel will close in on itself, its diameter getting smaller and smaller. You should have everyone do TAC rolls to notice "something" (while not telling them that the something they are rolling for is the tunnel).

The tunnel is getting smaller so slowly that it will be very difficult to notice until it is too small for a 7-foot tall Ancient Race adult to get into. The Coven will be able to Shapeshift themselves into something smaller (or turn themselves into Elementals and ooze their way through the smaller tunnel) and fly through the tunnel as it closes slowly. Here's the size/TAC TN guide:

- Shrunk to 6' diameter = TAC TN CRIT:1
- Shrunk to 5' diameter: TAC TN50
- Shrunk to 4' diameter: TAC TN40
- Shrunk to 3' diameter: TAC TN30
- Shrunk to 2' diameter: TAC TN20
- Shrunk to 1' diameter: TAC TN15
- Shrunk to 6 inches diameter: TAC TN10

You should do this over a couple dozen Phases while keeping them "distracted" by telling them something new about the thrones and the "sleeping" fey and all those details with every new TAC roll so they do not become suspicious until they actually notice that the tunnel has shrunk!

Remember the Cave does not allow Travel Magic to be used anywhere, so them getting out through the collapsing tunnel is paramount! Hopefully, they do, and this won't be the end of the Adventure... The Cave of Dreams is deadly, or weren't they warned?

SMALL BUCKETS OF WATER INTO WINE (TEMPTATION)

Somehow, the ambient blue glow from the walls are brighter in this room, such that everything is clearly seen. The whole room is square, about 50 feet to a side, but it is divided in front of you at the halfway mark by a transparent glass that stretches all the way to the ceiling 40 feet above and also all the way to each side wall. Before that dividing wall, on your side, is an ornate-looking glassy pedestal upon which sits a small glass goblet. Inside the rather thick glass wall, and running its whole length and height is a massive system of glass pipes and tubes and even small fires — it is obviously a very complicated alchemy lab of sorts. The convoluted distillation system ends with a small spigot that hovers directly over the glass goblet. In front and to the side of the pedestal is a small pile of what appear to be delicate items made of dust: there's a couple of rings, a boot, a necklace and a bracer.

On the other side of the wall, there are small pint-sized glass buckets that appear to be filled with water. Leaning up against the middle wall is a glass ladder that spans all the way to the ceiling where there is exactly one intake funnel. There is no way through the wall that you can see, and the way forward is on the other side of the wall!

This, mad-scientist type labyrinth of lab liquid piping is huge (40 feet high by 50 feet wide with a variety of fires for distillation in various places).

Have the players roll their Awareness or TAC for more info.

TN:20: There is one drop of white wine (you can tell by the smell) in the small glass goblet. There is enough only for one person to drink; it cannot be shared. This is, in fact, Dream Essence.

TN30: There are exactly (and this is extremely important): **the number of party members MINUS TWO** buckets on the other side the dream essence glass.

TAC TN20: The tubing spiraling piping down and out the small spigot to the wineglass is full of liquid (one can tell because of the bubbles in it), but not of sufficient weight to actually drip out of the pipe into the wineglass.

Sucking on the end of the spigot <u>will not</u> draw the liquid out.

If the party goes back and takes an alternate route, they might end up at a different "Temptation" but eventually, the labyrinth will wind back to this room, so there's no escaping it.

Solution

One person must drink the drop that is available in order to gain the ability to pass through the wall. They, and they alone, get to the other side and can take a bucket, climb up the ladder, and pour the contents of the bucket into the funnel. The system does its work, slowly, and finally out oozes just one more drop of the magical liquid, that the next person can drink in order to pass through the dream essence wall. They do this until there is no more water to pour (since all the buckets are now empty). Because there were exactly two buckets less than the number of party members (i.e., if there were all 10 party members, there would be only 8 buckets of water), there will be one party member still left on the entry-side of the middle glass wall. Herein lies the challenge.

Everything in this room is indestructible, the goblet, the walls the floor, ceiling, the spigot, the funnel, the buckets, everything — **except the glass ladder**, which will shatter if more than one person gets on it (or if it is hit hard by something).

Water, if used to refill a bucket (say by summoning a Water Elemental or from a canteen), will multiply nearly 600,000-fold, filling the room with water (it will not go out the open exit, so there is an escape, but anyone remaining in that side of the room without going out into the hall will have to swim (and could eventually drown (except for Karfyn, of course, who is immune to water and cannot drown)). It takes five filled pint-buckets of water to expand water all the way to the ceiling. After the water expands, the bucket will float on the water and have absolutely NO water in it. If a bucket is then used again to scoop water into it, the water multiplication (x600000 pints) will happen again with the same result: a dry bucket that does NOT hold water. That whole side of the room is 25' x 50' x 40' high, or 50,000 cubic feet. Thus, it takes approximately 374,026 gallons to fill it to the top, and so one pint-bucket of water multiplies into 74,805.2 gallons (or 598,441.6 pints). While this seems like overkill, the party might fuck up and end up leaving one party member behind even if they did not choose to do so, because once the room is filled with water, the buckets are automatically (and constantly) filled (since there's no air left for them to "choose" to be devoid of water). Also, the water pressure would compress constantly (because the buckets keep multiplying the water) so that no one except Karfyn would be able to be in the room (since the pressure would kill anyone else — you can also have the water become superheated if you like, because of the pressure. If you choose to do this, not even Karfyn will be able to enter it without a Defense vs. Fire (since Fire is effectively in the water as heat at that point)). *Note: these calculations are based on 8 pints to a gallon and 7.48 gallons to one cubic foot.*

So, the party has to come up with any liquid that is NOT water to put in an empty bucket in order to get the last person through. This can be done by [1] using ALTERATION:Transmute Liquid to Different Liquid spell to change the water they do have into a different liquid (and only after that pouring it into the bucket); [2] using their own piss or spittle (but this will take some time); [3] using their own blood (but this will have serious implications to the person pouring it into the funnel and to the person drinking the outcome (but it is the most fun!).

If they avoid using the bucket (which multiplies water), but

pour water directly into the funnel, they'll see that the funnel itself keeps water from entering it by some magical air lid that constantly disallows water to go down the funnel.

The party can use DIVINATION:Magical Diagnosis on the drop of liquid that came out of the spigot into the glass goblet. The divination will tell them it is Dream Essence that changes one living imbiber and anything non-living in his aura to Dream Essence for 2 phases so that it can meld into and pass through other things made of Dream Essence (like the glass). Moving into the other walls, floor or ceiling is possible, but those are much thicker than the Hexes of MVT a character has and so s/he would end up getting trapped in the "ice" of the Cave of Dreams.

A DreamCarver will know upon a TAC TN10 that the drop of liquid is some type of Dream Essence, and since it swirls around in the goblet like a real drop of liquid, it is beyond his ability to recreate (see DreamCarver Arcane fighting art power: Dream Essence on SC99; only creates "immovable objects").

100% Answer: Once at least one person is across (having drunk the first drop) and emptied at least one bucket into the funnel, use ALTERATION to increase the Size (volume) of the "water" originally in the buckets (it is actually hydrochloric acid) to be enough to fill a pint-bucket and pour the increase into the empty bucket, carefully to the same "brim" as all the bucket was originally filled. *Significant deviation from the precise measurement might result in 90% Answer effects.* If they did not think of this but did think of the "piss or spittle" answer, they can also use ALTERATION magic to Transmute the piss into the hydrochloric acid (they can know that it's acid by doing a Magical Diagnosis on the "water" in the buckets). Any liquid that isn't hydrochloric acid or blood will result in the 90% answer effects below. If the liquid is blood, go to the 80% answer. ***Note: ALTERATION has NO effect on the drop of Dream Essence in the goblet.***

90% Answer: all the party members that made it over so far must piss (or spit) into the bucket to make a pint. But any liquid other than the hydrochloric acid changes alchemy enough so that the imbiber can pass through the barrier but not any of their items...the person(s) drinking this piss/spit-solution will have all of their items turn to dust-items and fall off of them to the ground (when touched they will disintegrate). That is how the original dust items (a couple of rings, a boot, a necklace and a bracer) were there already! Someone else successfully navigated this room before they got here (and no doubt sits naked on one of the five Thrones)!

80% Answer (but more fun): add blood as liquid in bucket (but this makes blood magic for the next player to drink: FUN!!!! think of an effect and corruption). The person who pours the blood-tainted bucket into the alchemical system has a chance to become corrupted (splatter from the blood if s/he's not very careful: they must make their Balance check percentage otherwise accidentally cause the smallest of splatter while pouring (if they already broke the ladder and they're hovering or being held up by a human ladder, then assign a -5 Penalty to their roll). Blood will change the flames a different color as well as contaminate every clear pipe with bright red liquid as it progresses through the system (be sure to describe that!). The person drinking the "red wine" drop will be immediately corrupted 2% of his/her current MTAP (Mens Corruption). *They can, of course, pour the "red wine" out instead of drink it, and then come up with the 100% answer still at this point.*

Unless cleansed (Arvals have "Mens Healing" AR183), this corruption increases by 2% every 20 minutes (see below):

- in 2 hours and 40 minutes from imbibing → 10% Corrupted
- in 3 hours and 30 minutes from imbibing → 15% Corrupted
- in 4 hours and 20 minutes from imbibing → 20% Corrupted
- in 6 hours from imbibing → 30% Corrupted
- in 7 hours and 40 minutes from imbibing → 40% Corrupted
- in 9 hours and 20 minutes from imbibing → 50% Corrupted
- in 11 hours from imbibing → 60% Corrupted
- in 12 hours and 40 minutes from imbibing → 70% Corrupted
- in 14 hours and 20 minutes from imbibing → 80% Corrupted
- in 16 hours from imbibing → 90% Corrupted
- in 17 hours and 40 minutes → 100% Corrupted

(see Blood Magic Rules & WIL Checks on SC66). Thus it would be a GREAT idea for the last person NOT to be a Coven Member, especially if the party uses blood to fill the bucket/funnel. But this will yield some wonderfully fun role-playing even if the party has to kill the corrupted person before (at 100% corruption) they look to kill one of them! Remember, your Storyteller whims on corrupt actions should be more severe the more they become corrupted, and should be very subtle at first ("accidentally" (but the corrupted player really knows "purposely") pushing another player into the icy walls of the Cave (just to see what would happen), etc.). You can have a lot of fun with this. Some experienced players may know that the Blood mixed in with the magical alchemy has corrupted the person who drank it (and maybe the person who poured it, also). It will be up to him/her to tell (or not) what is really going on and thus work to cleanse the person (or not!).

Remember also that if the Corrupted individual casts a spell on anyone else, and the recipient lowers their resistance to that spell, and at least one point of POTency gets through, then that person will also be infected with corruption, and their corruption timeline will also start. It is thus possible for the entire party to become corrupted and then sit on the thrones. If this happens, you may want to give the Cave of Dreams an even more sinister character, and perhaps many more of the fey (once the Cave is opened and they are released) become monstrous instead of goody goodies who always obey and do what is nice. Thus, this could have far-reaching consequences in your game world.

FAIL Answer: actually selecting someone to sacrifice and stay behind. Or, in the alternative, being forced to leave someone be-

hind because they filled the buckets with water too many times and water is up to the ceiling.

Special Mention: Rangers with Animal Companions.

Should one of the Bonded Warriors be a Ranger or otherwise have a bonded animal companion, they will lose their companion at this point. But that is not to say the companion is dead. If they survive to the opening of the Cave, the animal companion will also be freed along with the Fey and they can be reunited (perhaps that can be the lead-into of another Adventure for the group: assisting the Ranger in finding his lost "puppy" wherever he detects the puppy is (probably an animal slave to a ruthless Wyrmkyn somewhere...)).

Grapes of Wrath (Temptation)

Reminding you of those Greek stories about the Minotaur in a Maze, you see below you a great stone maze stretching about a quarter of a mile across to where you can see a tiny opening which, no doubt, is the exit of the maze and of the room. It is below you because your current hallway opens up about 100 feet above the maze. The whole room is in the shape of a pentagon, which must mean you are getting close to the Cave of Dreams Throne Room. Though you cannot see into all of the maze corridors, even from this high up, you are pretty certain you also see no fey, no mino- taurs, no monsters patrolling the maze anywhere. It is empty ex- cept for the occasional lone skeleton of an outwitted maze walker.

Growing up the walls immediately to your right and left, and all around the pentagon, are grapevines as in harvest time: each of the vines is heavy with grapes. The vines themselves look like they might be able to support your weight also, but it would be an awfully long and slow climb to climb them horizontally on the wall just to get around to the exit. Perhaps the maze would be quicker, if only you could discover and memorize the path that leads to the exit.

Of course, flying might also be an option, unless magic is can- celed in this room. Wouldn't be a maze if you could just fly right over it. The thought makes you look down, just to see. Yes, good thing you looked. There are bones down there, along with the glint of metal — swords, armor perhaps — but certainly a panoply of fallen heroes, all broken on the stone maze below.

This room is just about as big as the Elemental War room. In fact, it is related. There are no elementals here, other than Ele- mental Spirit. In theory, each of the grapes houses yet another Elemental Spirit inside of itself, meaning emotion. And, ALL of the emotions are negative emotions.

If a party member eats a grape, they forfeit their MResist to the Elemental Spirit emotion, which has a POTency of 100L. If they break a grape on their way across to the other side or down to the maze, they get to roll their MResist against the Elemental Spirit (POT=100L) effects. Of course, Boreas will not be affected by any Elemental Spirit in this room.

The temptation here is to avoid turning on each other while

role-playing the elemental spirit's nuances perfectly. There is a base 30% chance every 10 feet that anyone climbing down or rappelling down (with their own rope, even) to the maze will burst at least one grape. And that is being careful!

Here's a list of negative Elemental Spirit emotions you can use (and of course you can choose your own); use a d5 two times if you want to roll them randomly::

1 on a d5
1. Anger
2. Hatred
3. Hopelessness
4. Self-Righteousness
5. Contempt

2 on a d5
1. Jealousy
2. Selfish ambition
3. Haughtiness (being overly smug about everything)
4. Paranoia about everyone and everything
5. Anger

3 on a d5
1. Envy
2. Selfish
3. Anger
4. Narcissistic
5. Holier than thou

4 on a d5
6. Doubtful about everything
7. Anger
8. Forgetful
9. Histrionic
10. Complainer about everything

5 on a d5
1. Irritable
2. Exhausted
3. Psychosomatic sickness (talking yourself into being ill)
4. Anger
5. Suspicious of everyone's true motives

As you can see, anger is the majority theme here, as the Cave is trying to get the party to turn on itself and kill each other. And it just might come to some fighting, but it will be Boreas's job to recognize what is happening and fix it as often as it happens.

100% Answer: Shapeshift into some type of bird and fly across to the exit. (Yes, it's that easy!) But seeing that Utility (flight) magic does not work, they may be discouraged from using a Shapeshifting magic to do this for fear it, too, would be canceled at some point.

95% Answer: Shapeshift into something so small that the odds of someone crushing a grape has a base chance of only 5% (mouse, for example), and climb down the vines to the maze, AFTER having discovered the maze path to the exit TAC TN40, and having memorized it: It's a Very Hard maze, to 2TN:5 minutes to memorize it, as long as they have a memorization slot (INT) available. To recall the solution, they will have to roll their Accuracy % when down in the maze. Grant an extra 20% bonus to

their roll if they Shapeshift into a 25-foot tall giant once down in the maze such that they can see over the 20-foot tall maze walls.

90% Answer: Climb down to the maze after memorizing the path to the exit (with all the party members memorizing it, in case one or more refuse (out of Anger or Forgetfulness, or Hopelessness, or whatever else) to "remember" the way out. Odds are that all of the part members (except Boreas) will have crushed a grape (they have 10 rolls to make) or eaten one by the time they are all the way down. It is possible for the affected to have to role-play more than one emotion (paranoia + complainer + narcissistic would probably prove hilarious!). Make sure to award on-the-spot Fortune Points for any outstanding role-playing of the Elemental Spirit afflictions!

They make it as a whole party (without anyone killing anyone) to the exit. As soon as they go through the exit and are in a hallway again, they will be free from the grapes' effects.

Also, award the party with some MenH-L/g items if they go down to the skeletons of other maze-goers. Not everything is bad news!

75% Answer: Climbing the whole way around the shortest distance on the pentagon laterally on the vines. Wow, they must already be really paranoid if they choose to do this instead of navigate the maze, especially after the hint we gave in the description that there are swords and armor down in the maze! This answer will no doubt take about two hours to do (that's a lot of climbing and a lot of grape crushing!). To make it easy, 20 grape-crushing possibilities per party member out to do the trick (at 30% chance each roll). They might not even make it all the way around before they end up falling to the maze anyway when attempting to kill each other (if role-played correctly). Boreas will have her hands full, and might run out of MTAP getting rid of all the magical effects.

Add 5% to any answer if the party casts MG/ML:Defense vs. Elemental Spirit at some point.

OPTIONAL: Encounters with other Adventurers

Want to add some fun to this challenge? Place some fucked-up, heavily-influenced (grape-intoxicated) adventurers you role-play down in the maze who have already turned on or murdered their own party members or were adventuring solo! Either way, can you imagine? "Hey you fucking bastard thief, give me back my sword!" REACTION. Be sure to have several wandering Personalities ready if you do this, along with more MenH items as rewards!

Note on % Answers.

You decide how much Experience the 100% Answer is worth. If they get that answer, they get 100% of the experience as group experience. Otherwise, they get less. You can add or deduct % points as you see fit to and from any answer (and come up with answers of your own; or they might come up with an answer nobody thought of yet!).

POOL OF DREAM SIGHT (TEMPTATION)

The icy hallway opens into perhaps the smallest cavern you've yet seen in the Cave of Dreams, though it is still large: it is round, at least 100 feet in diameter, with a rather pentagon-shaped pool of water in the center which fills almost the entire chamber. There is only about a two-foot wide walkway-ledge that goes all the way around the room to the exit; it protrudes out from the curving wall only about an inch above the water.

The water shimmers with all different colors of light, and is quite beautiful to look at, until you notice that the colors of light are actually moving images of reality. Deep, perhaps below??? the water you think you see a person sitting on a red crystal throne. The throne sitter's head is drooped, and they occasionally get struck by something akin to lightning every time the scene in the water changes to some other type of suffering or a person or group of people somewhere in the world. Could this be a dream you're looking at? A throne sitter's dream? Are the people in the dream the sitter's family or friends, perhaps?

Or is it real? Is this what they see while they're supposedly dreaming on the thrones? Suffering. Pain. Death. And to think that the Original Coven must sit the thrones, too, in order to fulfill Antara's prophecy, to undo the wicked magic she did?

Perhaps she should have sat the thrones instead of making other innocents do it. No one would want to sit on the thrones voluntarily, unless it was someone they loved on the throne. For who would condemn their friend to a potential eternity of this type of suffering: being forced to watch your friends and family suffer while there was nothing you could do to protect them, to stop them from suffering.

These thoughts could have made you angry were it not for clear and absolutely motionless water that seem to calm you down a bit. You have the feeling you wouldn't want the slightest ripple to disturb that calm, even though it would probably obscure the suffering images within it.

You suddenly realize that the ledge that was four feet wide is now only three feet wide, and it is disappearing inch by inch into the wall all the way around!

100% Answer: If the party starts immediately, half of them going left and half of them going right, they will all make it to the exit before the ledge is gone, without falling into the water. On their way around, they will notice four other throne sitters each "dreaming" their own horrible reality of suffering.

This whole room is a Wild-Magic Zone. Any casts (not triggered Anchored Spells, which remain unaffected) must be filtered/re-rolled through the Wild Magic Flowchart on SC116. The following Schools are exempted from the flowchart, however, and if you roll them, simply re-roll, as they do not function in this room: TRAvel, OFFensive, ALTeration.

This means that if they cast magic in this room, almost anything could happen: conjured fey showing up to battle them, spirits, elementals, a mundane item could be enchanted, a MenH item could be made non-magical (Destroy Binding), and so on, whatever the Wild Magic spell comes out to be.

If for any reason (falling, voluntarily entering, etc.) anyone touches or enters into the water, they immediately fall down into the water and get dropped out of the ceiling in the Cave of Dreams Throne Room, along with their Greater Doppelgänger who looks and thinks, and has all the same abilities, as they do, but only 75% of their Body Value (BV). If the Doppelgänger wins the battle, it will attempt to steal the Original Element, but in no wise will it ever sit on a throne! The doppelgänger(s) will immediately attack their counterpart(s) with wild abandon: "Only one of us may survive!"

The only way to avoid meeting their doppelgängers is to not touch the water, but to hurry across to the exit and run down the winding stairs that, after 50 feet (vertical distance, or 16 Hexes, which at 5 Hex MVT would take 3 Phases!) of spiraling down open into the Cave of Dream's Throne Room. Hopefully those who did not touch the water can get there before the doppelgänger(s) kill its/their party member(s)! If not, the doppelgänger(s) will act completely like and be indistinguishable from the party members.

{IF this happens, you should determine how many Phases it will take the party members who use the staircase to get to the Throne Room (we recommend THREE), based on their MVT rate. Then, you should ask them to step away while you conduct the doppelgänger fight(s) alone with only those who went through the water. Call them back only when [1] the three phases have passed or [2] one of them is killed (hopefully the doppelgänger). If [2], the group that took the stairs should not know which personality (the real party member or the doppelgänger) their fellow player is playing. *IF you want to add to the suspense, you can have the staircase group roll their Awareness to notice that two of the same person were seen down in the water...*}

90% Answer: If one gets sucked into the water, they should all go into the water. Yes, they'll all get doppelgängers but at least they will all know they have entities trying to become impostors. And, they'll be able to fight together (the Coven is always strongest when it is together!).

75% Answer: Running down the stairs when someone gets pulled into/through the water. OR: Going into the water voluntarily.

Casting magic that goes wild should not affect the % answer, as it only serves to increase the difficulty of the room.

THE THRONE ROOM

You hear the zapping sound before you even enter the Throne Room chamber. You're finally here, only to see the huge and ugly greensteel column ascending 50 feet above the center of all five red crystal thrones. Reddish purple pure negative energy lazily, mercilessly, zaps the throne sitters as if to electrocute them to death.

Indeed, the ones you can see (for the pentagon shape makes it impossible to see the other two throne sitters without walking around the center dais) are nearly naked, their clothing burned completely off by the negative energy.

With each zap, they cry out anew in agony.

Around the floor, hundreds, if not thousands of fey lie sleeping or dead. They seam to fill the many exits out of this room, going deeper into the Cave of Dreams as if this were only the beginning. The only exit they have not filled was the staircase. Perhaps that was added later, somehow, it leads you to think, but by whom?

This Throne Room is about the same size as the pentagon room with the pool directly above it. But it holds much more sorrow.

You suddenly realize you feel tired, but this is no Elemental Spirit effect, as Boreas appears to feel it too. The whole area seems to be draining you of your magical energy, a side effect of exposed greensteel, you now remember from your childhood stories of the Cave of Dreams. You've no time to waste!

At this point, describe also party members fighting what appear to be their identical twins, if that is going on. Or else, just have the doppelgänger party members act normally (no matter if they defeated the doppelgänger or not).

If there is no fighting going on, you can continue on with the description as they walk into and around the room, careful not to step on any of the fey, who are indeed alive, but sleeping, dreaming!

Careful not to hurt any of the fey, your examination of the throne sitters reveals their identities: Empress Maximina of the Astorian Empire, Ophelia Hadriana, Optimus Annius Verus, Emperor Scipio Julianus Astoricus Magnus (Maximina's brother!), and Queen Brûd of the Arkadians.

At Emperor Scipio's feet, and actually dead, is his secret lover, a Starborn (Celt) woman whom he came to rescue, although the party will probably not know any of that (it's just a spoiler for you so you know why he came to the Cave of Dreams in the first place, appointing his Sister to be Empress in his stead. Of course, when she found out he was trapped, she came to rescue him, but was deceived by his doppelgänger and sat on the wrong throne. Same thing happened to Optimus, who came next to rescue the Empress, then to Ophelia who came to rescue Optimus, and finally Queen Brûd, who came to rescue Ophelia, on whom she's had a lesbian crush for quite some time...

Now the doppelgängers were all ordered by He Who Stands Alone to sit the thrones (no way in hell they would do it otherwise) in order to deceive the Northern (Astorian) Empire so he could indeed place his Marune Minion on the Iron Throne (yes, Master Scholar Albanaeus Rufus was right all along: The Empress was a Marune Minion!).

Sitting The Thrones

Anyone who ascends the dais voluntarily with the intention of sitting a throne will suddenly lose control over themselves and be zapped by the pure negative energy coming from the greensteel column. They immediately pass out, and "time-phase" through the body sitting the throne while the body sitting the throne is "time-phased" off the throne down the dais, also still unconscious.

The reason for the unconsciousness is because the greensteel saps all their MTAP from them immediately, and coming off the throne and off the dais, there is still too much of a negative MTAP draw (on account of the Anti-magic zone the greensteel creates) for anyone to wake up.

While the prophecy states that the Original Coven must sit the thrones, the truth is that it's more important that the Original Elements each have a throne (no matter who sits the throne, as long as each throne gets its own Original Element). Thus, the Bonded Warriors are able to fulfill the prophecy as long as they kept their Bonded's Original Element, should the Coven Member have been killed along the way.

If they seat the thrones one after the other, they will notice that they did indeed free the previous sitter on the throne, but that they just slumped off and remained unconscious. Only when all five Original Elements sit all five thrones will there be enough power to temporarily stop the Anti-Magic Zone's negative draw.

When this happens, the strongest off the five to be set free, Maximina, the current Avatar of Astor, wakes within seconds of getting freed from the throne, and opens the Cave of Dreams, calling on her Avatar!

IT IS ENTIRELY POSSIBLE, however, for the party, especially if they are all corrupted, to go around and kill as many fey in the Throne Room as they can before their own life runs out (from the anti-magic draw) and they themselves fall unconscious....Just sayin'...

The Opening

As soon as the last member with the Original Element sits their thrones, there is a barely visible flash of light, and you can feel that the anti-magic aura of this room is gone. The snaky electric pure negative energy tentacles of the greensteel column no longer zap the sitters. But you surely don't know how long that will last!

Just as you were about to do something, anything, maybe even pull the sitters off the thrones, not giving any thought to whether you'd be the next one trapped thereon, you hear a moan...and then an angry groan.

It is none other than Empress Maximina, who is struggling to stand herself up, drained as she is.

At this point, wait to see what the players will do. Kill her? Hopefully no; hopefully they help her stand!

Her eyes wide open, she looks about the chamber, she sees her brother slouched at the base of the dais of his Throne. Suddenly, there's a fire in her eyes, literally, the sun, piercing through the clouds in her Skyborn Eyes. She takes a deep breath, then, at the top of her lungs, and so loud it could be thunder, she yells:

JULIAN!

no doubt calling upon her Avatar's Power, Julian Astor, who long before had joined the Presidium somewhere in the heavens.

Without warning, she streaks up as lightning directly through the roof of the Cave of Dreams! The lightning continues to thunder and then transforms into a slowly rotating light portal through which all of the sleeping fey — some now waking — are being lifted.

The other former sitters also start to wake. Emperor Scipio yells in agony as he lifts up a woman and carries her out through the portal, which ignores gravity with its gentle upward pull.

Once again, no one could know, not even Empress Maximina, how long the Cave of Dreams would thus bend under the intrusive power of the Immortal Empress.

It would be best to decide now what you're going to do. Shall you leave, too? Or shall you rescue someone from the fate of the red crystal thrones?

Here's the final decision. If the players want to keep their Coven, they may certainly do so by having their Bonded Warriors sit the thrones after them (or vice versa).

Unfortunately for them, though, the Original Elements were consumed and are no longer available to them. So, that means that the Original Coven, while certainly legendary, will no longer be immune to their own element, but will be as any other coven out there.

After the players have chosen which character to bring out of the Cave of Dreams, let them fly up and out the way all the other people/fey are doing: through the portal Maximina opened with Avatar-level magic.

And then congratulate them on a well-played (mostly) Adventure.

DENOUEMENT

You should, of course, have a ceremony in which the Empress will honor them, and perhaps confront and slay her doppelgänger right in front of their eyes. (Queen Brûd, Ophelia, Optimus, and Scipio will also have to find and slay their doppelgängers, which can be food for other adventures your players can go on...) One note about Scipio: he disappears only to be much later found suffering in Hades (he went off to kill He Who Stands Alone who lured his lover (now dead) to the Cave of Dreams, but LOST the duel!).

After the ceremony, at which they might be given estates, money, and even invited to secret societies (like the Flamine Order of Arvalis) as they are now trusted heroes of the Astorian and Arkadian empires. After all, the Arkadians can now come out of

hiding because they have their fey armies back! — yes, after all this, give them their long-awaited huge ADMIN SESSION and have fun awarding them experience, and be sure to include big fat goose eggs (ZEROES) for the stupid ideas they came up with.

Also, you should know that not all is good news. Along with the freed fey, the other twelve Marunes have been freed and are now free to work their evil in the world. They are called Those Who Run Together and will initially oppose He Who Stands Alone, until he convinces him that it was wholly Antara's fault why they got trapped in the Cave of Dreams...yeah right!

Sequel Adventures

You have several options and material now for sequels:

[1] Create a new story around one of the Marunes, He Who Makes Merry, creating the new pirate (and vampire) society on the hidden isle of Cilicia Nova.

[2] Hunt down the doppelgängers of the five current throne sitters and slay them (a doppelgänger is created by the Cave of Dreams every time someone sits a throne).

[3] Find out why the Dragons did not return with the faeries. Everyone thought the Cave of Dreams trapped them, too, but apparently not, since there were no dragons at all in the Cave and nor were any freed.

[4] Advocate for Master Scholar Albanaeus Rufus's exile to be rescinded (it's obviously not high on Empress Maximina's list of things to do).

[5] Discover and oppose how Senator Tullus Tullius tried to amass power against the Imperial Seat by uniting with the powerful Furia Tarquinia, who at this point would still be a very influential Rhodes instructor of alchemy. No one knows she is secretly the leader of the Cloud Dancer assassins! Not even Tullus.

Prequel Ideas

You could, of course, reveal a whole bunch of stuff you found out at the end towards the beginning and make adventures around that information that would lead into this Cave of Dreams adventure:

[1] Emperor Scipio has a secret Starborn (Celt) lover. And the Celts are looking at ways to exploit that to their advantage.

[2] Ophelia and Optimus are lovers; Queen Brûd, who is in hiding has been one of Ophelia's lovers under a different (shapeshifted guise) and is jealous. Bad things start happening to Optimus, and the adventurers are hired to be his bodyguards (they might even find out that he has gotten Ophelia pregnant at some point before he goes to rescue the Empress in the Cave of Dreams.

In any case, we thank you for buying this adventure and hope you and your players like it. We appreciate all the reviews left on Amazon, especially the great 5-Star ones, hint hint!

Sincerely,

The Subrosa.Games team

APPENDIX

IT'S YOUR SHOW...

As with most of our products, we've left several aspects of this adventure to your imagination. You're the Storyteller, and far be it from us to intrude on your style!

So, helps like maps, MenH items (though the ones we used are described), artifacts, side story threads, pics of personalities or fey, money chests, traps, etc., are all for you to go wild with. In case you didn't know, before the Sphere Tower war and subsequent Remaking of He Who Stands Alone, we use the map of the earth as it is in our own reality. Wyrmkyn Kyngdom is the entire expanse of the Ural mountain range. Arkadia (the mainland) is north in Pictland, though little pockets of Arkadia are scattered throughout the world. Astoria is the entire Roman Empire as it was under Augustus, with the Southern (Ammorian) Empire controlling Africa but not Aegyptus (which is an Astorian client kingdom/vassal). The rest of the earth has its own kingdoms all at the height of their power, as it stands to reason that in a reality where people can become immortal, the great men and women of legend would have continued their rule...

That being said, there are some adventure-specific things we've added here. And THAT being said, you're more than welcome to alter/change/dispose of them how you see fit! After all, it's your party and you know what's best for your players.

It's your show, after all!

True Spells Used in the Adventure

BLOOD SHAMAN

Shaman has Major Access to CUR/UTL; Standard Access to CHA/OFF; minor access to CON/DEF: MCTRL:24/48/72; has Tertiary Focus for CUR/OFF/UTL schools of magic; MAF4+MYS2 = 6d10 max POT

SHAMAN DRAIN (UTILITY - ANIMAL BLOOD)

5	Tertiary Focus
5	1 Being, Line of Sight + Self (0)
5	1d10+1 Phases
20	Being to Being MTAP Transfer (Victim to Self)
25	5d10+25 POTency (+5/die due to animal blood)
60	MTAP - 25% = **45 MTAP** for SK:Casting TN25

SHAMAN BLOODLETTING (CURATIVE - ANIMAL BLOOD)

5	Tertiary Focus
5	1 Being, Line of Sight
5	! extra Being Targeted, LOS
10	2d10 Forced Blood Flow (Blood Magic Option)
30	6d10+30 POTency (+5/die due to animal blood)
65	MTAP - 25% = **49 MTAP** for SK:Casting TN40

Blood Shaman usually has this spell anchored, so that if someone spills human blood (even his own), he will be able to take a Free Phase action and Trigger this spell, which allows all of his other spells to use

human blood as a source, which yields +10 POT/die instead of the animal blood bonus of +5 POT/die.

SHAMAN CHARM (CHARM)

10	No Focus
0	1 Being, Touched
3	1d10+1 Phases
7	Verbal Suggestion:Shouldn't: "SIT DOWN!" [10]
25	5d10+25 POTency
45	MTAP - 25% = **34 MTAP** for SK:Casting TN25

Shaman uses this when outnumbered to even the odds, or waits until someone gets too close.

SHAMAN CHARM 2 (CHARM)

10	No Focus
2	1 Being, Line of Sight
3	1d10+1 Phases
3	Verbal Suggestion:Why Not?: "Seek your friends' healing touch!" [5]
30	6d10+30 POTency
48	MTAP - 25% = **36 MTAP** for SK:Casting TN25

If the Shaman gets lucky enough for one of his victims to succumb to BLOODFIRE (below), Shaman Charm 2 could be very damaging to all of them. "Why Not?" is used because the victim would not know that the Bloodfire has a Contagious Effect.

SHAMAN BLOODFIRE (OFFENSIVE)

5	Tertiary Focus
5	1d5+1 Phases
0	1 Being, Line of Sight
0	Source: Blood
30	6d10+30 Killing Attack
+20	Contagious Effect
70	MTAP - 25% = **53 MTAP** for SK:Casting TN40

ORANK5 WYRMKYN WARRIORS

These Wyrmkyn have Major Access to CUR only with MCTRL:71 for Major Access; has No Foci for magic; MAF5+MYS2 = 7d10 max POT

BLOODLETTING (CURATIVE)

10	No Focus
5	1 Being, Line of Sight
1	Instantaneous
35	7d10 Forced Blood Flow (Blood Magic Option)
20	4d10 POT (+40 if there is already human blood)
71	MTAP - 25% = **54 MTAP** for SK:Casting TN40

Though these Wyrmkyn know this spell, since they only have a SK:-Casting of Rank 1, odds are they're never cast it, unless they have Fortune Points to use to buy extra d10s, so pay close attention if a player uses Fortune Points against them.

INCISION (CURATIVE)

10	No Focus
5	1 Being, Line of Sight
1	Instantaneous
10	Create Incision (2 BBV points)
30	6d10+30 POTency
56	MTAP - 25% = **42 MTAP** for SK:Casting TN25

ORANK7 WYRMKYN MANTIS

INCISION-FORCED BLOODLETTING (CURATIVE)

The Mantis of Tophyt has Major Access to CON/CUR/OFF; Standard Access to ATL/BEN; minor access to TIM: MCTRL:40/81/121; has Conjuring Artifact: Cimmeria; MAF7+MYS3 = 10d10 max POT

5	Tertiary Focus
5	1 Being, Line of Sight
20	+4 extra Beings Targeted, LOS
10	Choose My own Duration up to 7 Hours
25	Create Incisions x5
10	2d10 Forced Blood Flow (Blood Magic Option)
50	10d10 POTency (+10/die IF human blood there)
125	MTAP - 25% = **94 MTAP** for SK:Casting TN40

The Mantis always has this as an Anchored Spell, and will release it immediately upon entering combat in order to ensure there is human blood he can utilize for his Mantis powers and other spells.

BLOOD ELEMENTAL (CONJURATION)

30	No Gateway
-30	Have a Relic with conjuring qualities
3	Conjured stays for 1d10+7 Phases
30	Force 5 Lesser Destroyer Blood Elemental, Animal Form: Dinosaur (Tyrannosaurus Rex)
50	10d10 POTency +100 (+10/die human blood)
98	MTAP - 25% = **74 MTAP** for SK:Casting TN25

The Mantis conjures this creature (a real Tyrannosaurus Rex) from Cimmeria and infuses it with his blood magic to make it a terrifying blood elemental with corrupting qualities, as soon as there is enough human blood spilled to make it so: 1 point for each die of POTency (so 10 BBV points; remember, BBV is 60% of any blood wound).

His black gold ring is a Relic from Cimmeria, and takes 5d10 MTAP to activate with each Conjuration. One need not use Blood Magic to use it. What a cool find, huh? Perhaps someone else is looking for it....!

Coven Character Records: We did not fill in all the actual numbers because we wanted the players or you to customize & continue on with them in pencil. You/players can spend skill points & keep/spend X-Pts (see AR60). Each is Favored by Antara, which gives 5 [T] dice for any Skills, and +25 Luck daily use. There are other Trait bonuses & Talents you should ensure they look up and add. Coven Members use Guardian ORank bonuses (AR59).

Your True Spells

NAME:_____

NAME:_____

NAME:_____

NAME:_____

NAME:_____

NAME:_____

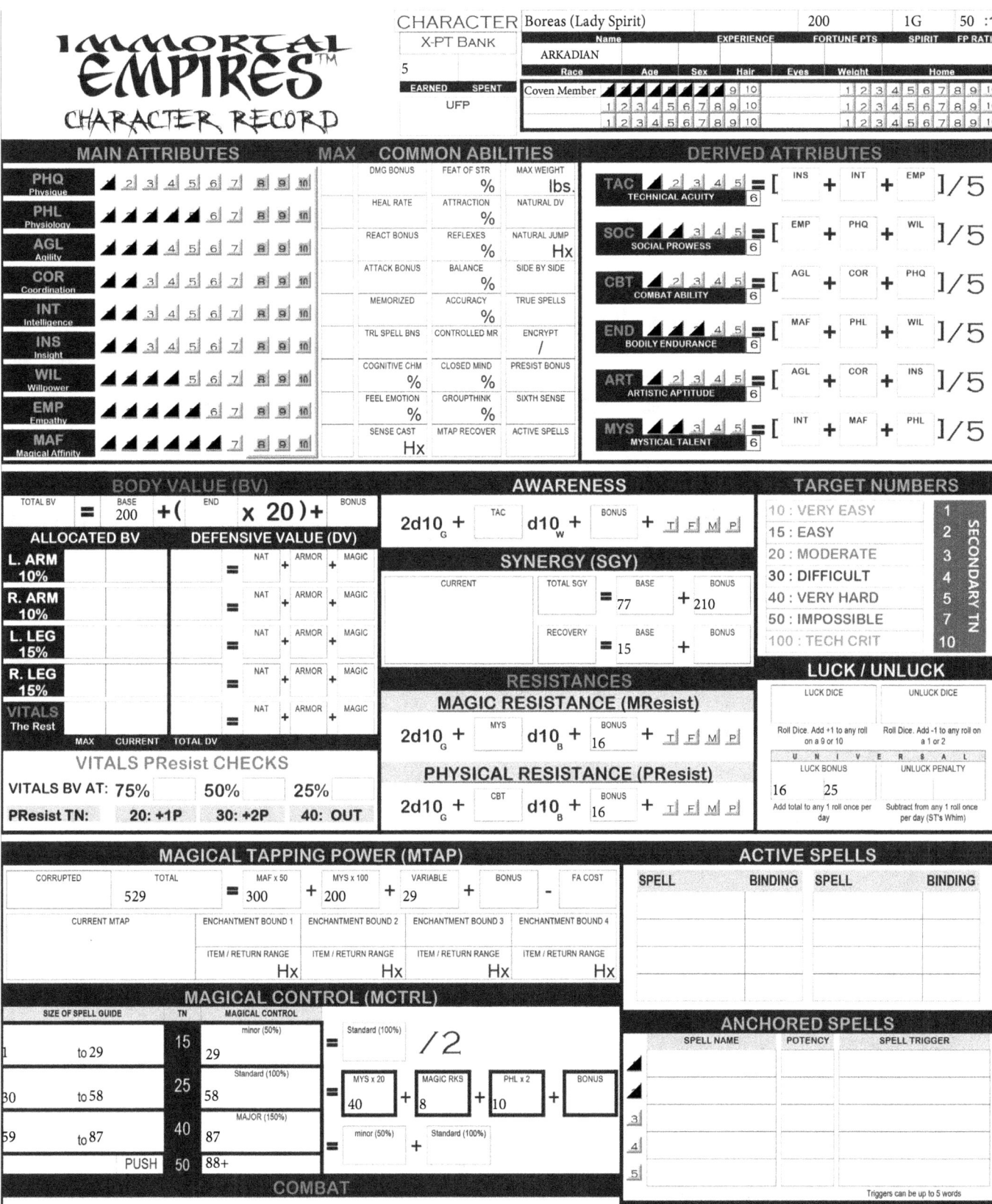

IMMORTAL EMPIRES™

SKILLS 1

200 Skill Points to spend Anywhere! Remember, each Rank costs its own number in Skill Points, and each Rank must be bought sequentially!

ACADEMIC/SCHOLARLY SKILLS

COST MODIFIER	
CATEGORY BONUS	TAC

GENERAL

- 1 2 3 4 5 T F M P *Administration*
- 1 2 3 4 5 T F M P *Business*
- 1 2 3 4 5 T F M P Appraising
- 1 2 3 4 5 T F M P Cartography
- 1 2 3 4 5 T F M P Engineering
- 1 2 3 4 5 T F M P Geography
- 1 2 3 4 5 T F M P History
- 1 2 3 4 5 T F M P Law
- 1 2 3 4 5 T F M P *Numbers*
- 1 2 3 4 5 T F M P Scribing
- 1 2 3 4 5 T F M P *Teaching*
- 1 2 3 4 5 T F M P Trade Lore

LANGUAGES

- 1 2 3 4 5 T F M P Ancient Races
- 1 2 3 4 5 T F M P Fey Races
- 1 2 3 4 5 T F M P Modern Races

MEDICINE

- 1 2 3 4 5 T F M P Chirurgy
- 1 2 3 4 5 T F M P *First Aid*
- 1 2 3 4 5 T F M P Gen. Medicine
- 1 2 3 4 5 T F M P Veterinary

SCIENCE

- 1 2 3 4 5 T F M P Astronomy
- 1 2 3 4 5 T F M P Biology
- 1 2 3 4 5 T F M P Forensics
- 1 2 3 4 5 T F M P Metallurgy
- 1 2 3 4 5 T F M P Metaphysics
- 1 2 3 4 5 T F M P Natural Earth

COMBAT/MILITARY SKILLS

COST MODIFIER	
CATEGORY BONUS	CBT

GENERAL

- 1 2 3 4 5 T F M P Footwork
- 1 2 3 4 5 T F M P Special Moves
- 1 2 3 4 5 T F M P Surprise

MINOR FIGHTING ARTS

- 1 2 3 4 5 T F M P Capua
- 1 2 3 4 5 T F M P E. S. Wrestling
- 1 2 3 4 5 T F M P Gladiator

TACTICS

- 1 2 3 4 5 T F M P Air
- 1 2 3 4 5 T F M P *Criminal*
- 1 2 3 4 5 T F M P Land
- 1 2 3 4 5 T F M P Magical
- 1 2 3 4 5 T F M P Naval

WEAPONRY

- 1 2 3 4 5 T F M P *Commoner*
- 1 2 3 4 5 T F M P Bows
- 1 2 3 4 5 T F M P Cleaving
- 1 2 3 4 5 T F M P Crossbows
- 1 2 3 4 5 T F M P Crushing
- 1 2 3 4 5 T F M P *Dodge*
- 1 2 3 4 5 T F M P Exotic
- 1 2 3 4 5 T F M P Long Blades
- 1 2 3 4 5 T F M P Martial
- 1 2 3 4 5 T F M P Polearms
- 1 2 3 4 5 T F M P Shields
- 1 2 3 4 5 T F M P Short Blades
- 1 2 3 4 5 T F M P Siege Engines
- 1 2 3 4 5 T F M P *Unarmed*

MAGICAL/MYSTICAL SKILLS

COST MODIFIER	
CATEGORY BONUS	MYS

GENERAL

- 1 2 3 4 5 T F M P Calligraphy
- 1 2 3 4 5 T F M P Herbalism
- 1 2 3 4 5 T F M P Leylines
- 1 2 3 4 5 T F M P Magical Theory
- 1 2 3 4 5 T F M P Philosophy

LORE

- 1 2 3 4 5 T F M P Arcane
- 1 2 3 4 5 T F M P Dimensions
- 1 2 3 4 5 T F M P Dragon
- 1 2 3 4 5 T F M P Faerie
- 1 2 3 4 5 T F M P Machine
- 1 2 3 4 5 T F M P Undead

MAGICAL

- 1 2 3 4 5 T F M P Candle Magic
- 1 2 3 4 5 ◢ F M P Casting
- 1 2 3 4 5 T F M P Centering
- 1 2 3 4 5 T F M P Constructs
- 1 2 3 4 5 T F M P Weave Celerity

MYSTICAL

- 1 2 3 4 5 T F M P Apothecary
- 1 2 3 4 5 T F M P Aura Reading
- 1 2 3 4 5 T F M P Counterspell
- 1 2 3 4 5 T F M P Hypnotism
- 1 2 3 4 5 T F M P Illusion
- 1 2 3 4 5 T F M P Pyrotechnics
- 1 2 3 4 5 T F M P Ritual Structures
- 1 2 3 4 5 T F M P Secret Rites
- 1 2 3 4 5 T F M P *Soothsaying*

Ancient Languages	Modern Languages
1)	1)
2)	2)
3)	3)
4)	4)
5)	5)

Fey Languages	Law
1)	1)
2)	2)
3)	3)
4)	4)
5)	5)

Geography	Engineering
1)	1)
2)	2)
3)	3)
4)	4)
5)	5)

Magical Access Chart

TRADITION:	Coven									
ALTERATION	◢ m S M	- m S M	- m S M	- m S M	- m S M
BENEDICTION	- m S ◢	- m S M	- m S M	- m S M	- m S M
CHARM	(orange)	- m S M	- m S M	- m S M	- m S M
CONJURING	- m S ◢	- m S M	- m S M	- m S M	- m S M
CURATIVE	(orange)	- m S M	- m S M	- m S M	- m S M
DEFENSIVE	- ◢ S M	- m S M	- m S M	- m S M	- m S M
DIVINATION	(orange)	- m S M	- m S M	- m S M	- m S M
ENCHANTING	- m S M	- m S M	- m S M	- m S M	- m S M
GLIMMERING	- m ◢ M	- m S M	- m S M	- m S M	- m S M
OFFENSIVE	◢ m S M	- m S M	- m S M	- m S M	- m S M
SHAPESHIFTING	- m ◢ M	- m S M	- m S M	- m S M	- m S M
TIME	- m S ◢	- m S M	- m S M	- m S M	- m S M
TRAVEL	- m ◢ M	- m S M	- m S M	- m S M	- m S M
UTILITY	- m ◢ M	- m S M	- m S M	- m S M	- m S M
WEATHER	(orange)	- m S M	- m S M	- m S M	- m S M

*Boreas can conjure ONLY Elemental Spirit

SKILLS 2

ARTISTIC/ARTISAN SKILLS

COST MODIFIER	
CATEGORY BONUS	ART

GENERAL
- 1 2 3 4 5 T F M P Cooking
- 1 2 3 4 5 T F M P Disable Apparatus
- 1 2 3 4 5 T F M P Disguise
- 1 2 3 4 5 T F M P Hand Talk
- 1 2 3 4 5 T F M P Lip Reading

ARTISTIC
- 1 2 3 4 5 T F M P Acting
- 1 2 3 4 5 T F M P Dancing
- 1 2 3 4 5 T F M P Forgery
- 1 2 3 4 5 T F M P Juggling
- 1 2 3 4 5 T F M P Lockpicking
- 1 2 3 4 5 T F M P Musical Comp.
- 1 2 3 4 5 T F M P Play Instrument
- 1 2 3 4 5 T F M P Paint/Draw
- 1 2 3 4 5 T F M P Poetry
- 1 2 3 4 5 T F M P Singing
- 1 2 3 4 5 T F M P Sleight of Hand
- 1 2 3 4 5 T F M P Voice Mimicry

TRADESKILL
- 1 2 3 4 5 T F M P
- 1 2 3 4 5 T F M P

SCHOLARLY ARTS
- 1 2 3 4 5 T F M P Bookbinding
- 1 2 3 4 5 T F M P Candlemaking
- 1 2 3 4 5 T F M P Glassblowing
- 1 2 3 4 5 T F M P Lapidary
- 1 2 3 4 5 T F M P Mus. Inst. Craft
- 1 2 3 4 5 T F M P Sculpting

OUTDOOR/ATHLETIC SKILLS

COST MODIFIER	
CATEGORY BONUS	END

GENERAL
- 1 2 3 4 5 T F M P Escape Bonds
- 1 2 3 4 5 T F M P Evasion
- 1 2 3 4 5 T F M P Rope Use
- 1 2 3 4 5 T F M P Stealth
- 1 2 3 4 5 T F M P Tracking

ANIMAL
- 1 2 3 4 5 T F M P Animal Handling
- 1 2 3 4 5 T F M P Animal Training
- 1 2 3 4 5 T F M P Riding, Aerial
- 1 2 3 4 5 T F M P Riding, Land
- 1 2 3 4 5 T F M P Riding, Sea Life
- 1 2 3 4 5 T F M P Zoology

ATHLETIC
- 1 2 3 4 5 T F M P Acrobatics
- 1 2 3 4 5 T F M P Charioteering
- 1 2 3 4 5 T F M P Climbing
- 1 2 3 4 5 T F M P Spelunking
- 1 2 3 4 5 T F M P Swimming

OUTDOOR
- 1 2 3 4 5 T F M P Camouflage
- 1 2 3 4 5 T F M P Trapping
- 1 2 3 4 5 T F M P Hunting
- 1 2 3 4 5 T F M P Horticulture
- 1 2 3 4 5 T F M P Meteorology
- 1 2 3 4 5 T F M P Navigation
- 1 2 3 4 5 T F M P Sailing, Lg. Craft
- 1 2 3 4 5 T F M P Sailing, Sm. Craft
- 1 2 3 4 5 T F M P Survival

SOCIAL/POLITICAL SKILLS

COST MODIFIER	
CATEGORY BONUS	SOC

GENERAL
- 1 2 3 4 5 T F M P Acquisition
- 1 2 3 4 5 T F M P Acumen
- 1 2 3 4 5 T F M P Games/Gambling
- 1 2 3 4 5 T F M P Interrogation
- 1 2 3 4 5 T F M P Intimidation
- 1 2 3 4 5 T F M P Lying
- 1 2 3 4 5 T F M P Savvy, Local
- 1 2 3 4 5 T F M P Savvy, Regional

POLITICAL
- 1 2 3 4 5 T F M P Bartering
- 1 2 3 4 5 T F M P Diplomacy
- 1 2 3 4 5 T F M P Oratory / Debate
- 1 2 3 4 5 T F M P Politics

SOCIAL
- 1 2 3 4 5 T F M P Crowdworking
- 1 2 3 4 5 T F M P Info. Gathering
- 1 2 3 4 5 T F M P Leadership
- 1 2 3 4 5 T F M P Mingling
- 1 2 3 4 5 T F M P Seduction

SOCIAL CIRCLES
- 1 2 3 4 5 T F M P Family
- 1 2 3 4 5 T F M P Social Classes

FAVOR BANK

TYPE	FAVORS	REQUESTS
SMALL		
BIG		
HUGE		
GUBERNATORIAL		
SENETORIAL		
ROYAL		
IMPERIAL		

EYES AND EARS

YOUR CLIENTS

NAME	BUSINESS	IMPORTANCE
PLOT	LOYALTY	WHERE	CLIENT PIN?

NAME	BUSINESS	IMPORTANCE
PLOT	LOYALTY	WHERE	CLIENT PIN?

NAME	BUSINESS	IMPORTANCE
PLOT	LOYALTY	WHERE	CLIENT PIN?

ENEMIES' CLIENTS

NAME	BUSINESS	IMPORTANCE
PLOT	LOYALTY	WHERE	CLIENT PIN?

NAME	BUSINESS	IMPORTANCE
PLOT	LOYALTY	WHERE	CLIENT PIN?

NAME	BUSINESS	IMPORTANCE
PLOT	LOYALTY	WHERE	CLIENT PIN?

PLOTS
A
B
C
D
E
F
G
H
I
J
K

ESTATES

NAME		LOCATION	VALUE	REVENUE
SOLDIERS	Gr. Champions	Champions	Elite	Above Average	Average	Below Average	Non-Military Population

NAME		LOCATION	VALUE	REVENUE
SOLDIERS	Gr. Champions	Champions	Elite	Above Average	Average	Below Average	Non-Military Population

MISCELLANEOUS

EQUIPMENT

PACK 1

ITEM	QTY.

PACK 2

ITEM	QTY.

PACK 3

ITEM	QTY.

PACK 4

ITEM	QTY.

Tiny Items such as vials stack up to 10 in the same slot, but mixing different small items in the same slot is not allowed. Thank you. --The Presidium

MONEY

CARRIED

GOLD	
SILVER	
COPPER	

1 GOLD = 25 SILVER = 100 COPPER

SPELL BATTERIES

POWER BASES

Power Base	Rating
Criminal	
Foreign	
Magical	
Military	
Political	
Popular	

ITEMS EQUIPPED

LOCATION	ITEM	DESCRIPTION
HEAD		
NECK		
TORSO		
ARMOR		
ARMS		
HANDS		
WAIST		
RING 1		
RING 2		
LEGS		
FEET		
BACK		
SHIELD		

COMPANIONS / BONDED ANIMALS

NAME					
PHQ		RACE		P Attk	
PHL		HGT		DMG	
AGL		WGT		M Attk	
COR		VOC		POT	
INT		RANK		PResist	
INS		AWARE		MResist	
WIL		MVT		BV	
EMP		DODGE		DV	
MAF		SGY		MTAP	
NAME					
PHQ		RACE		P Attk	
PHL		HGT		DMG	
AGL		WGT		M Attk	
COR		VOC		POT	
INT		RANK		PResist	
INS		AWARE		MResist	
WIL		MVT		BV	
EMP		DODGE		DV	
MAF		SGY		MTAP	

TRAITS / FLAWS

		MEMORIZED
PHYSICAL	+5 Natural Channeler, +3 Minor Aura, +1 Healthy (+3 BV Heal Rate)	
LEARNING	+5 Favored by Antara, +3 Spiritual Empath, +1 SK:Casting	
SOCIAL	+5 Daddy's Favorite, +3 Minor Allies I, +1 Bard	

FIGHTING ART POWERS

Physical	
Intellectual	
Spiritual	
Arcane	

HIRELINGS

SKILL PACKAGES

PACKAGE	RATIO
Coven Member	50 : 1
	: 1
	: 1
	: 1
	: 1
TOTAL	: 1

YOU select Boreas's Talents (Synergy), as a R8 Guardian (AR59 to see what she gets).

IMMORTAL EMPIRES™
CHARACTER RECORD

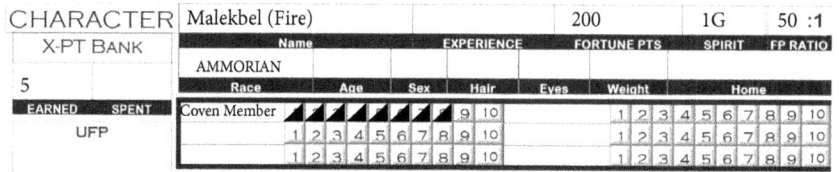

	Name	EXPERIENCE	FORTUNE PTS	SPIRIT	FP RATIO

X-PT BANK

5

EARNED   SPENT

UFP

Race	Age	Sex	Hair	Eyes	Weight	Home
AMMORIAN						
Coven Member			9	10		1 2 3 4 5 6 7 8 9 10
	1 2 3 4 5 6 7 8 9 10					1 2 3 4 5 6 7 8 9 10
	1 2 3 4 5 6 7 8 9 10					1 2 3 4 5 6 7 8 9 10

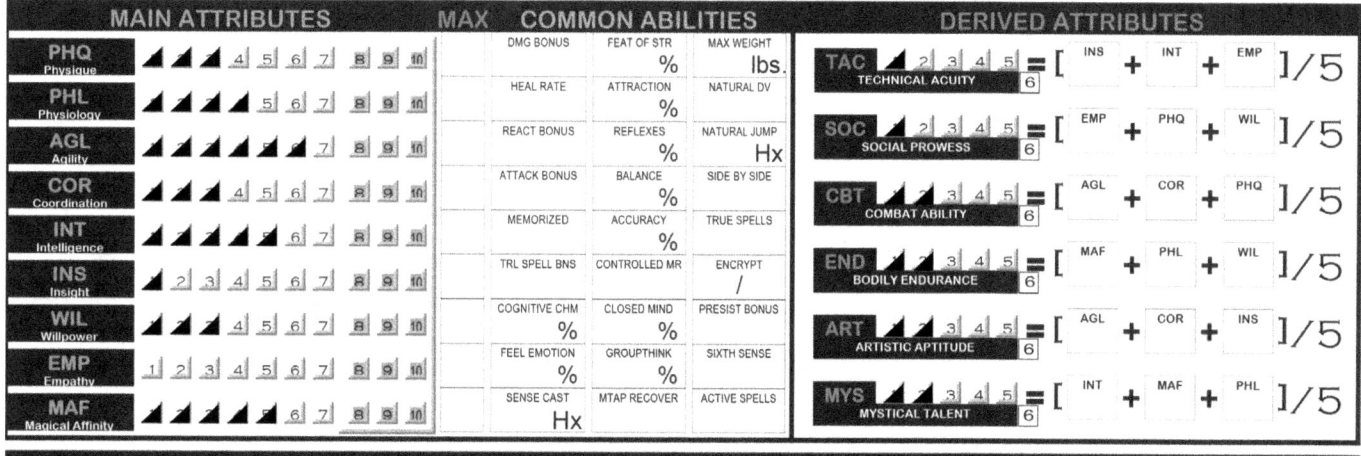

MAIN ATTRIBUTES — MAX

- PHQ Physique: 4 5 6 7 8 9 10
- PHL Physiology: 5 6 7 8 9 10
- AGL Agility: 7 8 9 10
- COR Coordination: 4 5 6 7 8 9 10
- INT Intelligence: 6 7 8 9 10
- INS Insight: 2 3 4 5 6 7 8 9 10
- WIL Willpower: 4 5 6 7 8 9 10
- EMP Empathy: 1 2 3 4 5 6 7 8 9 10
- MAF Magical Affinity: 6 7 8 9 10

COMMON ABILITIES

DMG BONUS	FEAT OF STR %	MAX WEIGHT lbs.
HEAL RATE	ATTRACTION %	NATURAL DV
REACT BONUS	REFLEXES %	NATURAL JUMP Hx
ATTACK BONUS	BALANCE %	SIDE BY SIDE
MEMORIZED	ACCURACY %	TRUE SPELLS
TRL SPELL BNS	CONTROLLED MR	ENCRYPT /
COGNITIVE CHM %	CLOSED MIND %	PRESIST BONUS
FEEL EMOTION %	GROUPTHINK %	SIXTH SENSE
SENSE CAST Hx	MTAP RECOVER	ACTIVE SPELLS

DERIVED ATTRIBUTES

- TAC TECHNICAL ACUITY: 2 3 4 5 / 6 = [INS + INT + EMP] 1/5
- SOC SOCIAL PROWESS: 2 3 4 5 / 6 = [EMP + PHQ + WIL] 1/5
- CBT COMBAT ABILITY: 3 4 5 / 6 = [AGL + COR + PHQ] 1/5
- END BODILY ENDURANCE: 3 4 5 / 6 = [MAF + PHL + WIL] 1/5
- ART ARTISTIC APTITUDE: 3 4 5 / 6 = [AGL + COR + INS] 1/5
- MYS MYSTICAL TALENT: 3 4 5 / 6 = [INT + MAF + PHL] 1/5

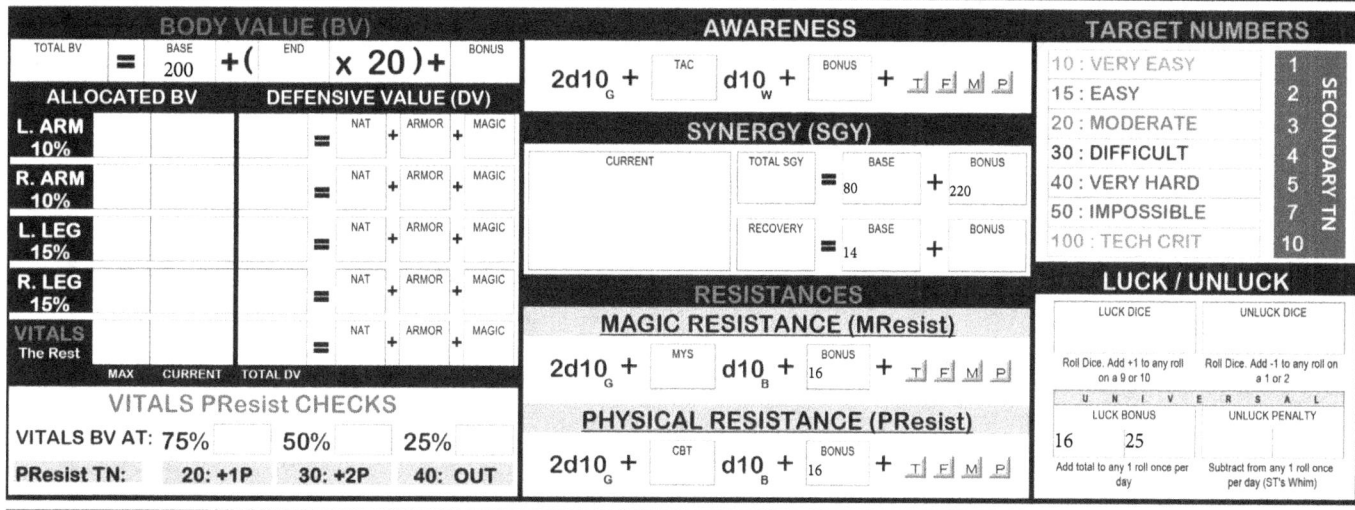

BODY VALUE (BV)

TOTAL BV	=	BASE 200	+(	END	x 20)+	BONUS

ALLOCATED BV — DEFENSIVE VALUE (DV)

		NAT	ARMOR	MAGIC
L. ARM 10%	=	NAT + ARMOR + MAGIC		
R. ARM 10%	=	NAT + ARMOR + MAGIC		
L. LEG 15%	=	NAT + ARMOR + MAGIC		
R. LEG 15%	=	NAT + ARMOR + MAGIC		
VITALS The Rest	=	NAT + ARMOR + MAGIC		

MAX   CURRENT   TOTAL DV

VITALS PResist CHECKS

VITALS BV AT: 75%   50%   25%

PResist TN: 20: +1P   30: +2P   40: OUT

AWARENESS

$2d10_G$ + TAC $d10_w$ + BONUS + T F M P

SYNERGY (SGY)

CURRENT	TOTAL SGY	=	BASE 80	+	BONUS 220
	RECOVERY	=	BASE 14	+	BONUS

RESISTANCES

MAGIC RESISTANCE (MResist)

$2d10_G$ + MYS $d10_B$ + BONUS 16 + T F M P

PHYSICAL RESISTANCE (PResist)

$2d10_G$ + CBT $d10_B$ + BONUS 16 + T F M P

TARGET NUMBERS

10 : VERY EASY	1
15 : EASY	2
20 : MODERATE	3
30 : DIFFICULT	4
40 : VERY HARD	5
50 : IMPOSSIBLE	7
100 : TECH CRIT	10

SECONDARY TN

LUCK / UNLUCK

LUCK DICE	UNLUCK DICE
Roll Dice. Add +1 to any roll on a 9 or 10	Roll Dice. Add -1 to any roll on a 1 or 2

UNIVERSAL

LUCK BONUS	UNLUCK PENALTY
16	25
Add total to any 1 roll once per day	Subtract from any 1 roll once per day (ST's Whim)

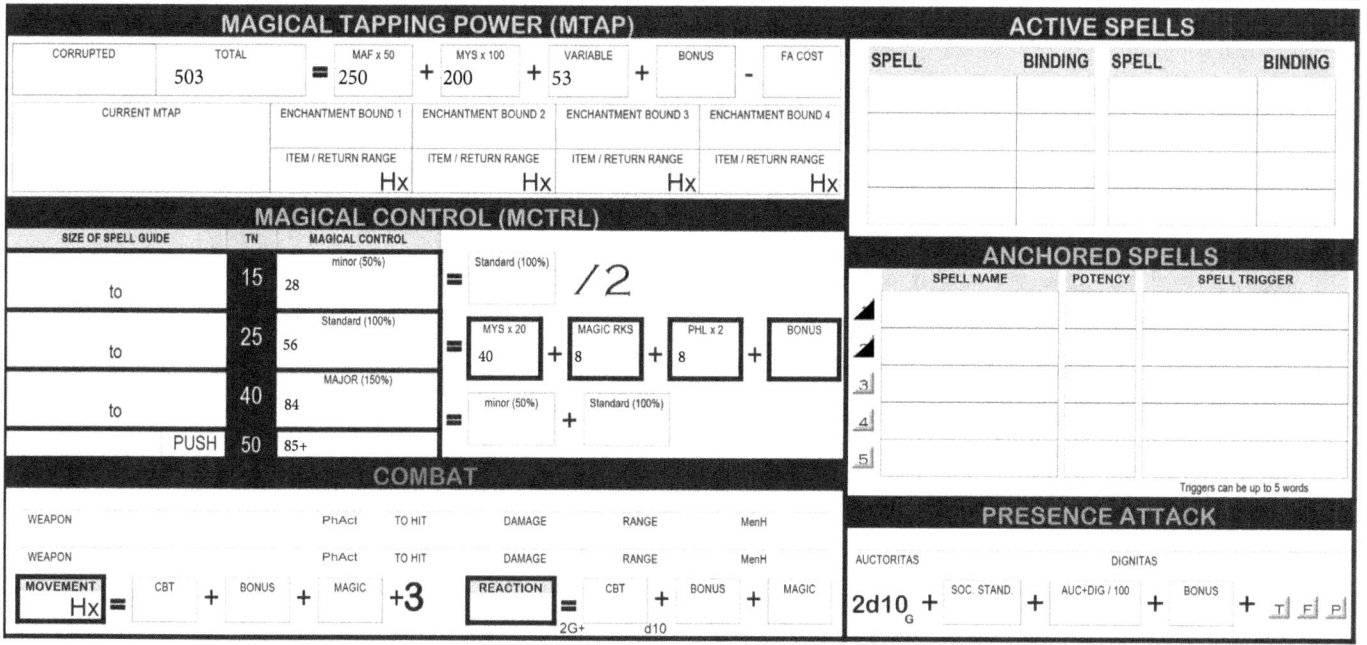

MAGICAL TAPPING POWER (MTAP)

CORRUPTED	TOTAL 503	=	MAF x 50 250	+	MYS x 100 200	+	VARIABLE 53	+	BONUS	FA COST -

CURRENT MTAP

ENCHANTMENT BOUND 1	ENCHANTMENT BOUND 2	ENCHANTMENT BOUND 3	ENCHANTMENT BOUND 4
ITEM / RETURN RANGE Hx	ITEM / RETURN RANGE Hx	ITEM / RETURN RANGE Hx	ITEM / RETURN RANGE Hx

MAGICAL CONTROL (MCTRL)

SIZE OF SPELL GUIDE	TN	MAGICAL CONTROL		
to	15	minor (50%) 28	=	Standard (100%) /2
to	25	Standard (100%) 56	=	MYS x 20 40 + MAGIC RKS 8 + PHL x 2 8 + BONUS
to	40	MAJOR (150%) 84	=	minor (50%) + Standard (100%)
PUSH	50	85+		

COMBAT

WEAPON		PhAct	TO HIT	DAMAGE	RANGE	MenH
WEAPON		PhAct	TO HIT	DAMAGE	RANGE	MenH

MOVEMENT Hx = CBT + BONUS + MAGIC +3

REACTION = CBT + BONUS + MAGIC   2G+   d10

ACTIVE SPELLS

SPELL	BINDING	SPELL	BINDING

ANCHORED SPELLS

	SPELL NAME	POTENCY	SPELL TRIGGER
1			
2			
3			
4			
5			

Triggers can be up to 5 words

PRESENCE ATTACK

AUCTORITAS	DIGNITAS	

$2d10_G$ + SOC. STAND. + AUC+DIG / 100 + BONUS + T F P

IMMORTAL EMPIRES™

SKILLS 1

200 Skill Points to spend Anywhere! Remember, each Rank costs its own number in Skill Points, and each Rank must be bought sequentially!

ACADEMIC/SCHOLARLY SKILLS

COST MODIFIER	
CATEGORY BONUS	
	TAC

GENERAL
Each entry: 1 2 3 4 5 T F M P

- Administration
- Business
- Appraising
- Cartography
- Engineering
- Geography
- History
- Law
- Numbers
- Scribing
- Teaching
- Trade Lore

LANGUAGES
- Ancient Races
- Fey Races
- Modern Races

MEDICINE
- Chirurgy
- First Aid
- Gen. Medicine
- Veterinary

SCIENCE
- Astronomy
- Biology
- Forensics
- Metallurgy
- Metaphysics
- Natural Earth

COMBAT/MILITARY SKILLS

COST MODIFIER	
CATEGORY BONUS	
	CBT

GENERAL
- Footwork
- Special Moves
- Surprise

MINOR FIGHTING ARTS
- Capua
- E. S. Wrestling
- Gladiator

TACTICS
- Air
- Criminal
- Land
- Magical
- Naval

WEAPONRY
- Commoner
- Bows
- Cleaving
- Crossbows
- Crushing
- Dodge
- Exotic
- Long Blades
- Martial
- Polearms
- Shields
- Short Blades
- Siege Engines
- Unarmed

MAGICAL/MYSTICAL SKILLS

COST MODIFIER	
CATEGORY BONUS	
	MYS

GENERAL
- Calligraphy
- Herbalism
- Leylines
- Magical Theory
- Philosophy

LORE
- Arcane
- Dimensions
- Dragon
- Faerie
- Machine
- Undead

MAGICAL
- Candle Magic
- Casting
- Centering
- Constructs
- Weave Celerity

MYSTICAL
- Apothecary
- Aura Reading
- Counterspell
- Hypnotism
- Illusion
- Pyrotechnics
- Ritual Structures
- Secret Rites
- Soothsaying

Ancient Languages	Modern Languages
1)	1)
2)	2)
3)	3)
4)	4)
5)	5)

Fey Languages	Law
1)	1)
2)	2)
3)	3)
4)	4)
5)	5)

Geography	Engineering
1)	1)
2)	2)
3)	3)
4)	4)
5)	5)

Magical Access Chart

TRADITION:	Coven			
ALTERATION	- m(✓) S M	- m S M	- m S M	- m S M
BENEDICTION	(orange)	- m S M	- m S M	- m S M
CHARM	- m S M(✓)	- m S M	- m S M	- m S M
CONJURING	- m S M(✓)	- m S M	- m S M	- m S M
CURATIVE	(orange)	- m S M	- m S M	- m S M
DEFENSIVE	(✓) m S M	- m S M	- m S M	- m S M
DIVINATION	(orange)	- m S M	- m S M	- m S M
ENCHANTING	(orange)	- m S M	- m S M	- m S M
GLIMMERING	- m S(✓) M	- m S M	- m S M	- m S M
OFFENSIVE	- m S M(✓)	- m S M	- m S M	- m S M
SHAPESHIFTING	- m S(✓) M	- m S M	- m S M	- m S M
TIME	(✓) m S M	- m S M	- m S M	- m S M
TRAVEL	- (✓) S M	- m S M	- m S M	- m S M
UTILITY	- m S(✓) M	- m S M	- m S M	- m S M
WEATHER	(orange)	- m S M	- m S M	- m S M

*Malekbel can conjure ONLY Fire Elementals

IMMORTAL EMPIRES™

SKILLS 2

ARTISTIC/ARTISAN SKILLS	OUTDOOR/ATHLETIC SKILLS	SOCIAL/POLITICAL SKILLS
COST MODIFIER	COST MODIFIER	COST MODIFIER
CATEGORY BONUS — ART	CATEGORY BONUS — END	CATEGORY BONUS — SOC

ARTISTIC/ARTISAN SKILLS

GENERAL
- 1 2 3 4 5 T F M P Cooking
- 1 2 3 4 5 T F M P Disable Apparatus
- 1 2 3 4 5 T F M P Disguise
- 1 2 3 4 5 T F M P Hand Talk
- 1 2 3 4 5 T F M P Lip Reading

ARTISTIC
- 1 2 3 4 5 T F M P Acting
- 1 2 3 4 5 T F M P Dancing
- 1 2 3 4 5 T F M P Forgery
- 1 2 3 4 5 T F M P Juggling
- 1 2 3 4 5 T F M P Lockpicking
- 1 2 3 4 5 T F M P Musical Comp.
- 1 2 3 4 5 T F M P Play Instrument
- 1 2 3 4 5 T F M P Paint/Draw
- 1 2 3 4 5 T F M P Poetry
- 1 2 3 4 5 T F M P Singing
- 1 2 3 4 5 T F M P Sleight of Hand
- 1 2 3 4 5 T F M P Voice Mimicry

TRADESKILL
- 1 2 3 4 5 T F M P
- 1 2 3 4 5 T F M P

SCHOLARLY ARTS
- 1 2 3 4 5 T F M P Bookbinding
- 1 2 3 4 5 T F M P Candlemaking
- 1 2 3 4 5 T F M P Glassblowing
- 1 2 3 4 5 T F M P Lapidary
- 1 2 3 4 5 T F M P Mus. Inst. Craft
- 1 2 3 4 5 T F M P Sculpting

OUTDOOR/ATHLETIC SKILLS

GENERAL
- 1 2 3 4 5 T F M P Escape Bonds
- 1 2 3 4 5 T F M P Evasion
- 1 2 3 4 5 T F M P Rope Use
- 1 2 3 4 5 T F M P Stealth
- 1 2 3 4 5 T F M P Tracking

ANIMAL
- 1 2 3 4 5 T F M P Animal Handling
- 1 2 3 4 5 T F M P Animal Training
- 1 2 3 4 5 T F M P Riding, Aerial
- 1 2 3 4 5 T F M P Riding, Land
- 1 2 3 4 5 T F M P Riding, Sea Life
- 1 2 3 4 5 T F M P Zoology

ATHLETIC
- 1 2 3 4 5 T F M P Acrobatics
- 1 2 3 4 5 T F M P Charioteering
- 1 2 3 4 5 T F M P Climbing
- 1 2 3 4 5 T F M P Spelunking
- 1 2 3 4 5 T F M P Swimming

OUTDOOR
- 1 2 3 4 5 T F M P Camouflage
- 1 2 3 4 5 T F M P Trapping
- 1 2 3 4 5 T F M P Hunting
- 1 2 3 4 5 T F M P Horticulture
- 1 2 3 4 5 T F M P Meteorology
- 1 2 3 4 5 T F M P Navigation
- 1 2 3 4 5 T F M P Sailing, Lg. Craft
- 1 2 3 4 5 T F M P Sailing, Sm. Craft
- 1 2 3 4 5 T F M P Survival

SOCIAL/POLITICAL SKILLS

GENERAL
- 1 2 3 4 5 T F M P Acquisition
- 1 2 3 4 5 T F M P Acumen
- 1 2 3 4 5 T F M P Games/Gambling
- 1 2 3 4 5 T F M P Interrogation
- 1 2 3 4 5 T F M P Intimidation
- 1 2 3 4 5 T F M P Lying
- 1 2 3 4 5 T F M P Savvy, Local
- 1 2 3 4 5 T F M P Savvy, Regional

POLITICAL
- 1 2 3 4 5 T F M P Bartering
- 1 2 3 4 5 T F M P Diplomacy
- 1 2 3 4 5 T F M P Oratory / Debate
- 1 2 3 4 5 T F M P Politics

SOCIAL
- 1 2 3 4 5 T F M P Crowdworking
- 1 2 3 4 5 T F M P Info. Gathering
- 1 2 3 4 5 T F M P Leadership
- 1 2 3 4 5 T F M P Mingling
- 1 2 3 4 5 T F M P Seduction

SOCIAL CIRCLES
- 1 2 3 4 5 T F M P Family
- 1 2 3 4 5 T F M P Social Classes
- 1 2 3 4 5 T F M P
- 1 2 3 4 5 T F M P
- 1 2 3 4 5 T F M P

FAVOR BANK

TYPE	FAVORS	REQUESTS
SMALL		
BIG		
HUGE		
GUBERNATORIAL		
SENETORIAL		
ROYAL		
IMPERIAL		

EYES AND EARS

YOUR CLIENTS

NAME	BUSINESS	IMPORTANCE
PLOT	LOYALTY	WHERE	CLIENT PIN?
NAME	BUSINESS	IMPORTANCE
PLOT	LOYALTY	WHERE	CLIENT PIN?
NAME	BUSINESS	IMPORTANCE
PLOT	LOYALTY	WHERE	CLIENT PIN?

ENEMIES' CLIENTS

NAME	BUSINESS	IMPORTANCE
PLOT	LOYALTY	WHERE	CLIENT PIN?
NAME	BUSINESS	IMPORTANCE
PLOT	LOYALTY	WHERE	CLIENT PIN?
NAME	BUSINESS	IMPORTANCE
PLOT	LOYALTY	WHERE	CLIENT PIN?

PLOTS

A
B
C
D
E
F
G
H
I
J
K

ESTATES

NAME	LOCATION	VALUE	REVENUE
SOLDIERS	Gr. Champions	Champions	Elite	Above Average	Average	Below Average	Non-Military Population
NAME	LOCATION	VALUE	REVENUE
SOLDIERS	Gr. Champions	Champions	Elite	Above Average	Average	Below Average	Non-Military Population

MISCELLANEOUS

EQUIPMENT

PACK 1

ITEM	QTY.

PACK 2

ITEM	QTY.

PACK 3

ITEM	QTY.

PACK 4

ITEM	QTY.

Tiny Items such as vials stack up to 10 in the same slot, but mixing different small items in the same slot is not allowed. Thank you. --The Presidium

MONEY

CARRIED

GOLD	
SILVER	
COPPER	

1 GOLD = 25 SILVER = 100 COPPER

SPELL BATTERIES

POWER BASES

Power Base	Rating
Criminal	
Foreign	
Magical	
Military	
Political	
Popular	

ITEMS EQUIPPED

LOCATION	ITEM	DESCRIPTION
HEAD		
NECK		
TORSO		
ARMOR		
ARMS		
HANDS		
WAIST		
RING 1		
RING 2		
LEGS		
FEET		
BACK		
SHIELD		

COMPANIONS / BONDED ANIMALS

NAME					
PHQ		RACE		P Attk	
PHL		HGT		DMG	
AGL		WGT		M Attk	
COR		VOC		POT	
INT		RANK		PResist	
INS		AWARE		MResist	
WIL		MVT		BV	
EMP		DODGE		DV	
MAF		SGY		MTAP	
NAME					
PHQ		RACE		P Attk	
PHL		HGT		DMG	
AGL		WGT		M Attk	
COR		VOC		POT	
INT		RANK		PResist	
INS		AWARE		MResist	
WIL		MVT		BV	
EMP		DODGE		DV	
MAF		SGY		MTAP	

TRAITS / FLAWS

		MEMORIZED
PHYSICAL	+5 Grace Under Fire, +3 Sensual, +1 Fast (+3 MVT Rate)	
LEARNING	+5 Favored by Antara, +3 Burner, +1 SK:Dodge	
SOCIAL	+5 Well-connected, +3 Talented Sycophant, +1 Player	

FIGHTING ART POWERS

Physical	
Intellectual	
Spiritual	
Arcane	

HIRELINGS

SKILL PACKAGES

PACKAGE	RATIO
Coven Member	50 : 1
	: 1
	: 1
	: 1
	: 1
TOTAL	: 1

YOU select Malekbel's Talents (Synergy), as a R8 Guardian (AR59 to see what he gets).

IMMORTAL EMPIRES™
CHARACTER RECORD

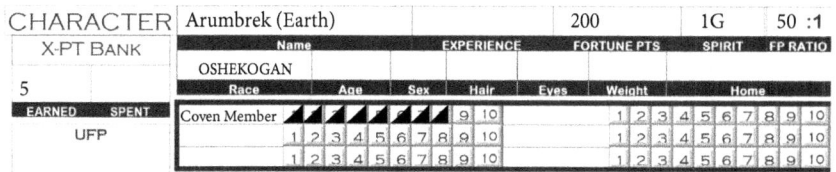

CHARACTER	Arumbrek (Earth)		200	1G	50 :1
X-PT BANK	Name	EXPERIENCE	FORTUNE PTS	SPIRIT	FP RATIO
5	OSHEKOGAN				
EARNED SPENT	Race	Age	Sex	Hair	Eyes	Weight	Home
UFP	Coven Member	9	10			1 2 3 4 5 6 7 8 9 10
	1 2 3 4 5 6 7 8 9 10				1 2 3 4 5 6 7 8 9 10
	1 2 3 4 5 6 7 8 9 10				1 2 3 4 5 6 7 8 9 10

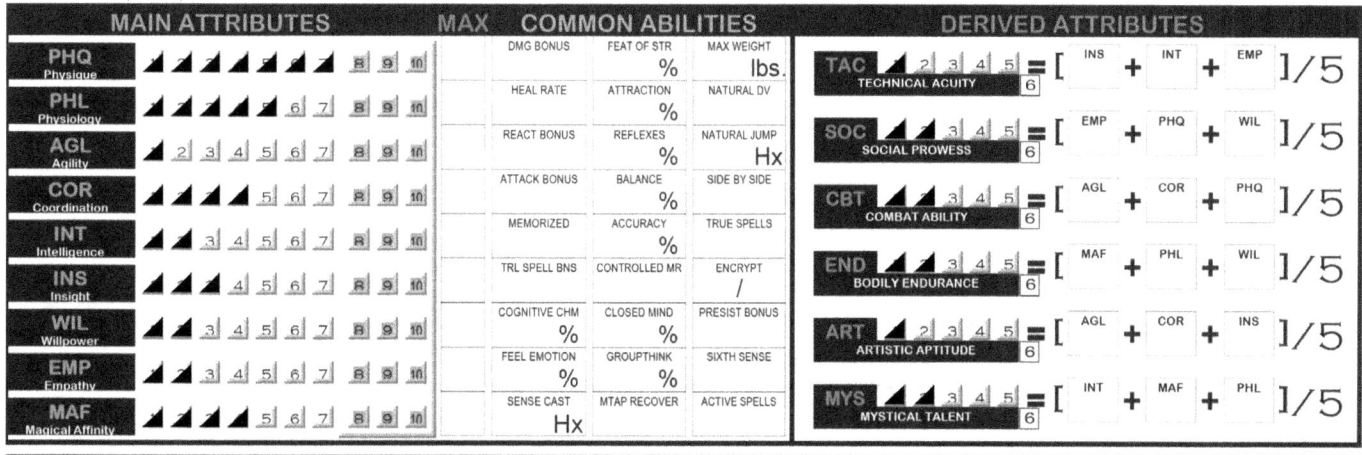

MAIN ATTRIBUTES

Attribute		Values
PHQ	Physique	8 9 10
PHL	Physiology	6 7 8 9 10
AGL	Agility	2 3 4 5 6 7 8 9 10
COR	Coordination	5 6 7 8 9 10
INT	Intelligence	3 4 5 6 7 8 9 10
INS	Insight	4 5 6 7 8 9 10
WIL	Willpower	3 4 5 6 7 8 9 10
EMP	Empathy	3 4 5 6 7 8 9 10
MAF	Magical Affinity	5 6 7 8 9 10

MAX — COMMON ABILITIES

DMG BONUS	FEAT OF STR %	MAX WEIGHT lbs.
HEAL RATE	ATTRACTION %	NATURAL DV
REACT BONUS	REFLEXES %	NATURAL JUMP Hx
ATTACK BONUS	BALANCE %	SIDE BY SIDE
MEMORIZED	ACCURACY %	TRUE SPELLS
TRL SPELL BNS	CONTROLLED MR	ENCRYPT /
COGNITIVE CHM %	CLOSED MIND %	PRESIST BONUS
FEEL EMOTION %	GROUPTHINK %	SIXTH SENSE
SENSE CAST Hx	MTAP RECOVER	ACTIVE SPELLS

DERIVED ATTRIBUTES

TAC TECHNICAL ACUITY	2 3 4 5 = 6	[INS + INT + EMP] /5
SOC SOCIAL PROWESS	3 4 5 = 6	[EMP + PHQ + WIL] /5
CBT COMBAT ABILITY	3 4 5 = 6	[AGL + COR + PHQ] /5
END BODILY ENDURANCE	3 4 5 = 6	[MAF + PHL + WIL] /5
ART ARTISTIC APTITUDE	2 3 4 5 = 6	[AGL + COR + INS] /5
MYS MYSTICAL TALENT	3 4 5 = 6	[INT + MAF + PHL] /5

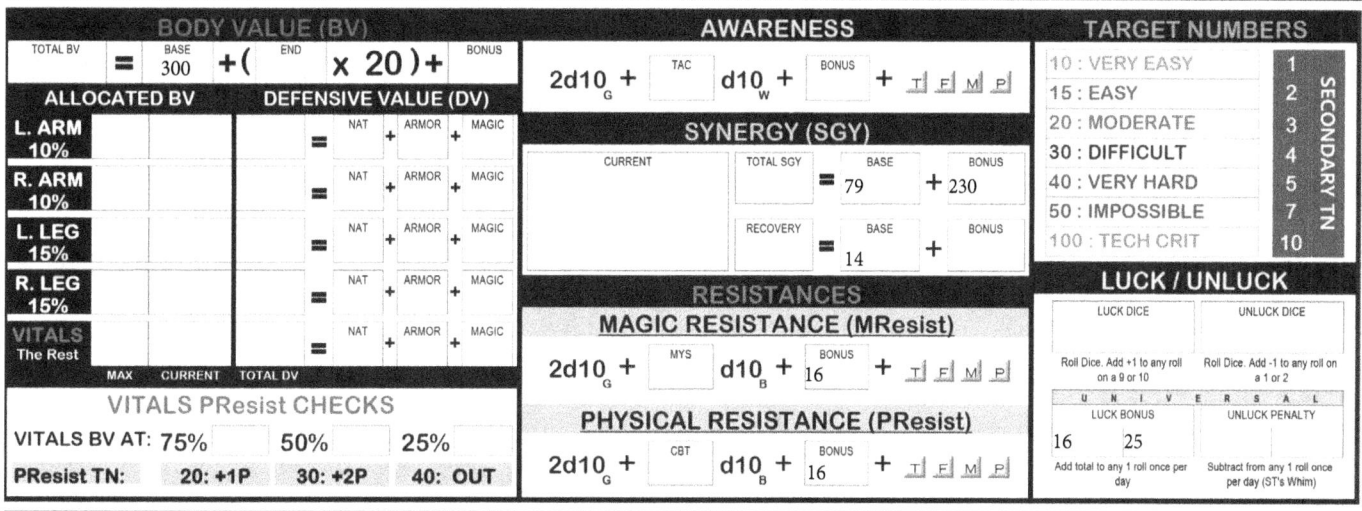

BODY VALUE (BV)

TOTAL BV	=	BASE 300	+(	END x 20)+	BONUS

ALLOCATED BV | DEFENSIVE VALUE (DV)

	ALLOCATED BV		= NAT + ARMOR + MAGIC
L. ARM 10%		=	NAT + ARMOR + MAGIC
R. ARM 10%		=	NAT + ARMOR + MAGIC
L. LEG 15%		=	NAT + ARMOR + MAGIC
R. LEG 15%		=	NAT + ARMOR + MAGIC
VITALS The Rest		=	NAT + ARMOR + MAGIC

MAX   CURRENT   TOTAL DV

VITALS PResist CHECKS

VITALS BV AT: 75%   50%   25%

PResist TN: 20: +1P   30: +2P   40: OUT

AWARENESS

2d10 G + [TAC] d10 W + [BONUS] + T F M P

SYNERGY (SGY)

CURRENT	TOTAL SGY = 79	BASE + BONUS 230
	RECOVERY = 14	BASE + BONUS

RESISTANCES

MAGIC RESISTANCE (MResist)

2d10 G + [MYS] d10 B + [BONUS 16] + T F M P

PHYSICAL RESISTANCE (PResist)

2d10 G + [CBT] d10 B + [BONUS 16] + T F M P

TARGET NUMBERS

10 : VERY EASY	1
15 : EASY	2
20 : MODERATE	3
30 : DIFFICULT	4
40 : VERY HARD	5
50 : IMPOSSIBLE	7
100 : TECH CRIT	10

SECONDARY TN

LUCK / UNLUCK

LUCK DICE	UNLUCK DICE
Roll Dice. Add +1 to any roll on a 9 or 10	Roll Dice. Add -1 to any roll on a 1 or 2

UNIVERSAL

LUCK BONUS	UNLUCK PENALTY
16 25	
Add total to any 1 roll once per day	Subtract from any 1 roll once per day (ST's Whim)

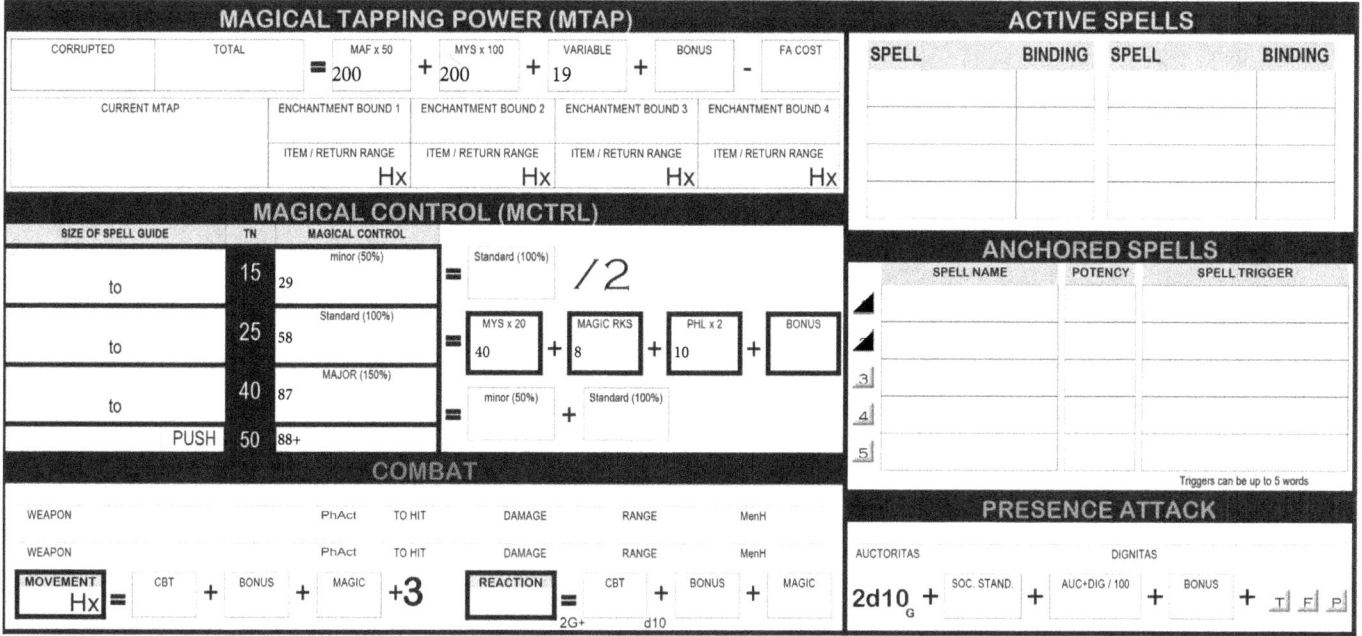

MAGICAL TAPPING POWER (MTAP)

CORRUPTED	TOTAL	= MAF x 50 200	+ MYS x 100 200	+ VARIABLE 19	+ BONUS	- FA COST

CURRENT MTAP	ENCHANTMENT BOUND 1	ENCHANTMENT BOUND 2	ENCHANTMENT BOUND 3	ENCHANTMENT BOUND 4
	ITEM / RETURN RANGE Hx	ITEM / RETURN RANGE Hx	ITEM / RETURN RANGE Hx	ITEM / RETURN RANGE Hx

MAGICAL CONTROL (MCTRL)

SIZE OF SPELL GUIDE	TN	MAGICAL CONTROL
to	15	minor (50%) 29
to	25	Standard (100%) 58
to	40	MAJOR (150%) 87
PUSH	50	88+

Standard (100%) = /2

= MYS x 20 40 + MAGIC RKS 8 + PHL x 2 10 + BONUS

= minor (50%) + Standard (100%)

ACTIVE SPELLS

SPELL	BINDING	SPELL	BINDING

ANCHORED SPELLS

SPELL NAME	POTENCY	SPELL TRIGGER
3		
4		
5		

Triggers can be up to 5 words

COMBAT

WEAPON	PhAct	TO HIT	DAMAGE	RANGE	MenH
WEAPON	PhAct	TO HIT	DAMAGE	RANGE	MenH

MOVEMENT Hx	= CBT + BONUS + MAGIC +3	REACTION = CBT + BONUS + MAGIC
		2G+ d10

PRESENCE ATTACK

AUCTORITAS		DIGNITAS	
2d10 G + SOC. STAND. + AUC+DIG / 100 + BONUS + T F P

IMMORTAL EMPIRES™

SKILLS 1

200 Skill Points to spend Anywhere! Remember, each Rank costs its own number in Skill Points, and each Rank must be bought sequentially!

ACADEMIC/SCHOLARLY SKILLS

COST MODIFIER	
CATEGORY BONUS	
	TAC

GENERAL

- 1 2 3 4 5 T F M P *Administration*
- 1 2 3 4 5 T F M P *Business*
- 1 2 3 4 5 T F M P Appraising
- 1 2 3 4 5 T F M P Cartography
- 1 2 3 4 5 T F M P Engineering
- 1 2 3 4 5 T F M P Geography
- 1 2 3 4 5 T F M P History
- 1 2 3 4 5 T F M P Law
- 1 2 3 4 5 T F M P *Numbers*
- 1 2 3 4 5 T F M P Scribing
- 1 2 3 4 5 T F M P *Teaching*
- 1 2 3 4 5 T F M P Trade Lore

LANGUAGES

- 1 2 3 4 5 T F M P Ancient Races
- 1 2 3 4 5 T F M P Fey Races
- 1 2 3 4 5 T F M P Modern Races

MEDICINE

- 1 2 3 4 5 T F M P Chirgury
- 1 2 3 4 5 T F M P *First Aid*
- 1 2 3 4 5 T F M P Gen. Medicine
- 1 2 3 4 5 T F M P Veterinary

SCIENCE

- 1 2 3 4 5 T F M P Astronomy
- 1 2 3 4 5 T F M P Biology
- 1 2 3 4 5 T F M P Forensics
- 1 2 3 4 5 T F M P Metallurgy
- 1 2 3 4 5 T F M P Metaphysics
- 1 2 3 4 5 T F M P Natural Earth

COMBAT/MILITARY SKILLS

COST MODIFIER	
CATEGORY BONUS	
	CBT

GENERAL

- 1 2 3 4 5 T F M P Footwork
- 1 2 3 4 5 T F M P Special Moves
- 1 2 3 4 5 T F M P Surprise

MINOR FIGHTING ARTS

- 1 2 3 4 5 T F M P Capua
- 1 2 3 4 5 T F M P E. S. Wrestling
- 1 2 3 4 5 T F M P Gladiator

TACTICS

- 1 2 3 4 5 T F M P Air
- 1 2 3 4 5 T F M P *Criminal*
- 1 2 3 4 5 T F M P Land
- 1 2 3 4 5 T F M P Magical
- 1 2 3 4 5 T F M P Naval

WEAPONRY

- 1 2 3 4 5 T F M P *Commoner*
- 1 2 3 4 5 T F M P Bows
- 1 2 3 4 5 T F M P Cleaving
- 1 2 3 4 5 T F M P Crossbows
- 1 2 3 4 5 T F M P Crushing
- 1 2 3 4 5 T F M P *Dodge*
- 1 2 3 4 5 T F M P Exotic
- 1 2 3 4 5 T F M P Long Blades
- 1 2 3 4 5 T F M P Martial
- 1 2 3 4 5 T F M P Polearms
- 1 2 3 4 5 T F M P Shields
- 1 2 3 4 5 T F M P Short Blades
- 1 2 3 4 5 T F M P Siege Engines
- 1 2 3 4 5 T F M P *Unarmed*

MAGICAL/MYSTICAL SKILLS

COST MODIFIER	
CATEGORY BONUS	
	MYS

GENERAL

- 1 2 3 4 5 T F M P Calligraphy
- 1 2 3 4 5 T F M P Herbalism
- 1 2 3 4 5 T F M P Leylines
- 1 2 3 4 5 T F M P Magical Theory
- 1 2 3 4 5 T F M P Philosophy

LORE

- 1 2 3 4 5 T F M P Arcane
- 1 2 3 4 5 T F M P Dimensions
- 1 2 3 4 5 T F M P Dragon
- 1 2 3 4 5 T F M P Faerie
- 1 2 3 4 5 T F M P Machine
- 1 2 3 4 5 T F M P Undead

MAGICAL

- 1 2 3 4 5 T F M P Candle Magic
- 1 2 3 4 5 T F M P Casting
- 1 2 3 4 5 T F M P Centering
- 1 2 3 4 5 T F M P Constructs
- 1 2 3 4 5 T F M P Weave Celerity

MYSTICAL

- 1 2 3 4 5 T F M P Apothecary
- 1 2 3 4 5 T F M P Aura Reading
- 1 2 3 4 5 T F M P Counterspell
- 1 2 3 4 5 T F M P Hypnotism
- 1 2 3 4 5 T F M P Illusion
- 1 2 3 4 5 T F M P Pyrotechnics
- 1 2 3 4 5 T F M P Ritual Structures
- 1 2 3 4 5 T F M P Secret Rites
- 1 2 3 4 5 T F M P *Soothsaying*

Ancient Languages	Modern Languages
1)	1)
2)	2)
3)	3)
4)	4)
5)	5)

Fey Languages	Law
1)	1)
2)	2)
3)	3)
4)	4)
5)	5)

Geography	Engineering
1)	1)
2)	2)
3)	3)
4)	4)
5)	5)

Magical Access Chart

TRADITION:	Coven				
ALTERATION	- m S M	- m S M	- m S M	- m S M	- m S M
BENEDICTION		- m S M	- m S M	- m S M	- m S M
CHARM		- m S M	- m S M	- m S M	- m S M
CONJURING	- m S M	- m S M	- m S M	- m S M	- m S M
CURATIVE	- m S M	- m S M	- m S M	- m S M	- m S M
DEFENSIVE	- m S M	- m S M	- m S M	- m S M	- m S M
DIVINATION		- m S M	- m S M	- m S M	- m S M
ENCHANTING		- m S M	- m S M	- m S M	- m S M
GLIMMERING	m S M	- m S M	- m S M	- m S M	- m S M
OFFENSIVE	- S M	- m S M	- m S M	- m S M	- m S M
SHAPESHIFTING	- m S M	- m S M	- m S M	- m S M	- m S M
TIME	- m S M	- m S M	- m S M	- m S M	- m S M
TRAVEL	m S M	- m S M	- m S M	- m S M	- m S M
UTILITY	- m S M	- m S M	- m S M	- m S M	- m S M
WEATHER		- m S M	- m S M	- m S M	- m S M

*Arumbrek can conjure ONLY Earth Elementals

SKILLS 2

ARTISTIC/ARTISAN SKILLS

COST MODIFIER	
CATEGORY BONUS	
	ART

GENERAL

1 2 3 4 5	T F M P	Cooking
1 2 3 4 5	T F M P	Disable Apparatus
1 2 3 4 5	T F M P	Disguise
1 2 3 4 5	T F M P	Hand Talk
1 2 3 4 5	T F M P	Lip Reading

ARTISTIC

1 2 3 4 5	T F M P	Acting
1 2 3 4 5	T F M P	Dancing
1 2 3 4 5	T F M P	Forgery
1 2 3 4 5	T F M P	Juggling
1 2 3 4 5	T F M P	Lockpicking
1 2 3 4 5	T F M P	Musical Comp.
1 2 3 4 5	T F M P	Play Instrument
1 2 3 4 5	T F M P	Paint/Draw
1 2 3 4 5	T F M P	Poetry
1 2 3 4 5	T F M P	Singing
1 2 3 4 5	T F M P	Sleight of Hand
1 2 3 4 5	T F M P	Voice Mimicry

TRADESKILL

1 2 3 4 5	T F M P	
1 2 3 4 5	T F M P	

SCHOLARLY ARTS

1 2 3 4 5	T F M P	Bookbinding
1 2 3 4 5	T F M P	Candlemaking
1 2 3 4 5	T F M P	Glassblowing
1 2 3 4 5	T F M P	Lapidary
1 2 3 4 5	T F M P	Mus. Inst. Craft
1 2 3 4 5	T F M P	Sculpting

OUTDOOR/ATHLETIC SKILLS

COST MODIFIER	
CATEGORY BONUS	
	END

GENERAL

1 2 3 4 5	T F M P	Escape Bonds
1 2 3 4 5	T F M P	Evasion
1 2 3 4 5	T F M P	Rope Use
1 2 3 4 5	T F M P	Stealth
1 2 3 4 5	T F M P	Tracking

ANIMAL

1 2 3 4 5	T F M P	Animal Handling
1 2 3 4 5	T F M P	Animal Training
1 2 3 4 5	T F M P	Riding, Aerial
1 2 3 4 5	T F M P	Riding, Land
1 2 3 4 5	T F M P	Riding, Sea Life
1 2 3 4 5	T F M P	Zoology

ATHLETIC

1 2 3 4 5	T F M P	Acrobatics
1 2 3 4 5	T F M P	Charioteering
1 2 3 4 5	T F M P	Climbing
1 2 3 4 5	T F M P	Spelunking
1 2 3 4 5	T F M P	Swimming

OUTDOOR

1 2 3 4 5	T F M P	Camouflage
1 2 3 4 5	T F M P	Trapping
1 2 3 4 5	T F M P	Hunting
1 2 3 4 5	T F M P	Horticulture
1 2 3 4 5	T F M P	Meteorology
1 2 3 4 5	T F M P	Navigation
1 2 3 4 5	T F M P	Sailing, Lg. Craft
1 2 3 4 5	T F M P	Sailing, Sm. Craft
1 2 3 4 5	T F M P	Survival

SOCIAL/POLITICAL SKILLS

COST MODIFIER	
CATEGORY BONUS	
	SOC

GENERAL

1 2 3 4 5	T F M P	Acquisition
1 2 3 4 5	T F M P	Acumen
1 2 3 4 5	T F M P	Games/Gambling
1 2 3 4 5	T F M P	Interrogation
1 2 3 4 5	T F M P	Intimidation
1 2 3 4 5	T F M P	Lying
1 2 3 4 5	T F M P	Savvy, Local
1 2 3 4 5	T F M P	Savvy, Regional

POLITICAL

1 2 3 4 5	T F M P	Bartering
1 2 3 4 5	T F M P	Diplomacy
1 2 3 4 5	T F M P	Oratory / Debate
1 2 3 4 5	T F M P	Politics

SOCIAL

1 2 3 4 5	T F M P	Crowdworking
1 2 3 4 5	T F M P	Info. Gathering
1 2 3 4 5	T F M P	Leadership
1 2 3 4 5	T F M P	Mingling
1 2 3 4 5	T F M P	Seduction

SOCIAL CIRCLES

1 2 3 4 5	T F M P	Family
1 2 3 4 5	T F M P	Social Classes
1 2 3 4 5	T F M P	
1 2 3 4 5	T F M P	
1 2 3 4 5	T F M P	

FAVOR BANK

TYPE	FAVORS	REQUESTS
SMALL		
BIG		
HUGE		
GUBERNATORIAL		
SENETORIAL		
ROYAL		
IMPERIAL		

EYES AND EARS

YOUR CLIENTS

NAME	BUSINESS	IMPORTANCE
PLOT	LOYALTY	WHERE	CLIENT PIN?

NAME	BUSINESS	IMPORTANCE
PLOT	LOYALTY	WHERE	CLIENT PIN?

NAME	BUSINESS	IMPORTANCE
PLOT	LOYALTY	WHERE	CLIENT PIN?

ENEMIES' CLIENTS

NAME	BUSINESS	IMPORTANCE
PLOT	LOYALTY	WHERE	CLIENT PIN?

NAME	BUSINESS	IMPORTANCE
PLOT	LOYALTY	WHERE	CLIENT PIN?

NAME	BUSINESS	IMPORTANCE
PLOT	LOYALTY	WHERE	CLIENT PIN?

PLOTS

A
B
C
D
E
F
G
H
I
J
K

ESTATES

NAME	LOCATION	VALUE	REVENUE
SOLDIERS	Gr. Champions	Champions	Elite	Above Average	Average	Below Average	Non-Military Population

NAME	LOCATION	VALUE	REVENUE
SOLDIERS	Gr. Champions	Champions	Elite	Above Average	Average	Below Average	Non-Military Population

MISCELLANEOUS

EQUIPMENT

PACK 1

ITEM	QTY.

PACK 2

ITEM	QTY.

PACK 3

ITEM	QTY.

PACK 4

ITEM	QTY.

Tiny Items such as vials stack up to 10 in the same slot, but mixing different small items in the same slot is not allowed. Thank you. --The Presidium

MONEY

CARRIED

GOLD	
SILVER	
COPPER	

1 GOLD = 25 SILVER = 100 COPPER

SPELL BATTERIES

POWER BASES

Power Base	Rating
Criminal	
Foreign	
Magical	
Military	
Political	
Popular	

ITEMS EQUIPPED

LOCATION	ITEM	DESCRIPTION
HEAD		
NECK		
TORSO		
ARMOR		
ARMS		
HANDS		
WAIST		
RING 1		
RING 2		
LEGS		
FEET		
BACK		
SHIELD		

COMPANIONS / BONDED ANIMALS

NAME				
PHQ		RACE		P Attk
PHL		HGT		DMG
AGL		WGT		M Attk
COR		VOC		POT
INT		RANK		PResist
INS		AWARE		MResist
WIL		MVT		BV
EMP		DODGE		DV
MAF		SGY		MTAP

NAME				
PHQ		RACE		P Attk
PHL		HGT		DMG
AGL		WGT		M Attk
COR		VOC		POT
INT		RANK		PResist
INS		AWARE		MResist
WIL		MVT		BV
EMP		DODGE		DV
MAF		SGY		MTAP

TRAITS / FLAWS

PHYSICAL	+5 Superior Body Type, +3 Naturally Tough Skin, +1 Well Balanced
LEARNING	+5 Favored by Antara, +3 Trivia Genius, +1 SK:Crushing Weapons
SOCIAL	+5 Royal Favorite, +3 Wealthy, +1 E.F. Hutton Syndrome

MEMORIZED

FIGHTING ART POWERS

Physical	
Intellectual	
Spiritual	
Arcane	

HIRELINGS

SKILL PACKAGES

PACKAGE	RATIO
Coven Member	50 : 1
	: 1
	: 1
	: 1
	: 1
TOTAL	: 1

YOU select Arumbrek's Talents (Synergy), as a R8 Guardian (AR59 to see what he gets).

IMMORTAL EMPIRES™
CHARACTER RECORD

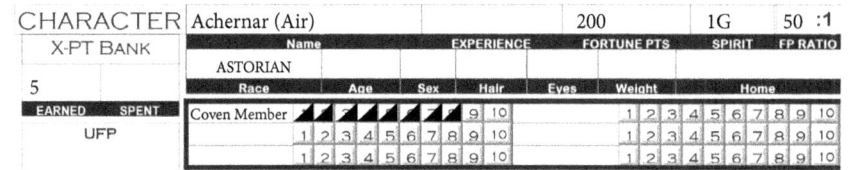

CHARACTER	Achernar (Air)		200	1G	50 :1
X-PT BANK		Name	EXPERIENCE	FORTUNE PTS	SPIRIT · FP RATIO
5	ASTORIAN				
EARNED · SPENT	Race	Age · Sex · Hair	Eyes · Weight	Home	
UFP	Coven Member	9 · 10	1 2 3 4 5 6 7 8 9 10		
	1 2 3 4 5 6 7 8 9 10		1 2 3 4 5 6 7 8 9 10		
	1 2 3 4 5 6 7 8 9 10		1 2 3 4 5 6 7 8 9 10		

MAIN ATTRIBUTES MAX · COMMON ABILITIES · DERIVED ATTRIBUTES

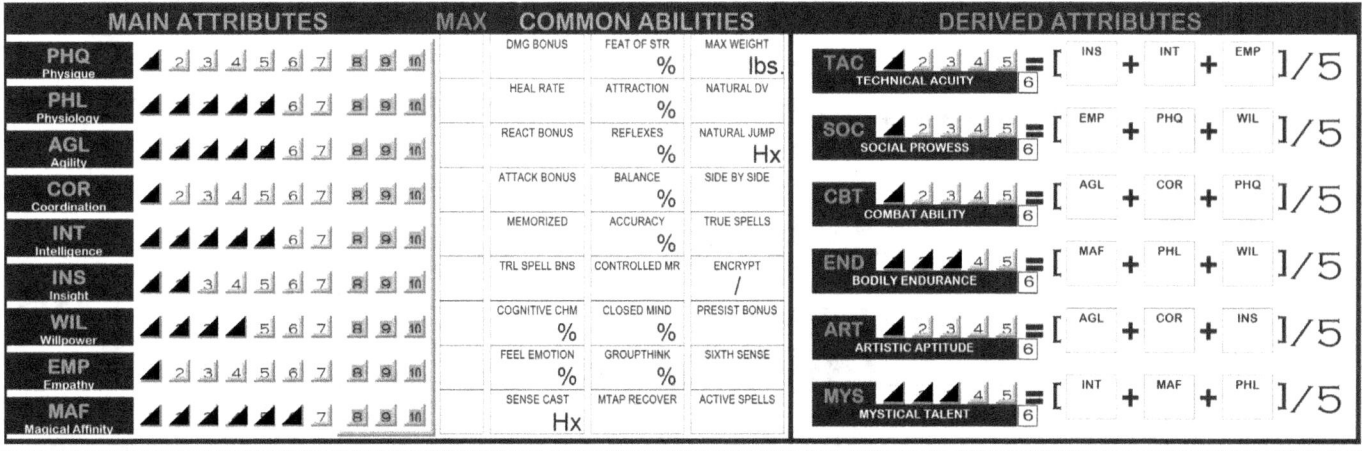

MAIN ATTRIBUTES

- PHQ — Physique
- PHL — Physiology
- AGL — Agility
- COR — Coordination
- INT — Intelligence
- INS — Insight
- WIL — Willpower
- EMP — Empathy
- MAF — Magical Affinity

COMMON ABILITIES

DMG BONUS	FEAT OF STR	MAX WEIGHT lbs.
HEAL RATE	ATTRACTION %	NATURAL DV
REACT BONUS	REFLEXES %	NATURAL JUMP Hx
ATTACK BONUS	BALANCE %	SIDE BY SIDE
MEMORIZED	ACCURACY %	TRUE SPELLS
TRL SPELL BNS	CONTROLLED MR	ENCRYPT /
COGNITIVE CHM %	CLOSED MIND %	PRESIST BONUS
FEEL EMOTION %	GROUPTHINK %	SIXTH SENSE
SENSE CAST Hx	MTAP RECOVER	ACTIVE SPELLS

DERIVED ATTRIBUTES

- TAC — TECHNICAL ACUITY: 6 = [INS + INT + EMP] / 5
- SOC — SOCIAL PROWESS: 6 = [EMP + PHQ + WIL] / 5
- CBT — COMBAT ABILITY: 6 = [AGL + COR + PHQ] / 5
- END — BODILY ENDURANCE: 6 = [MAF + PHL + WIL] / 5
- ART — ARTISTIC APTITUDE: 6 = [AGL + COR + INS] / 5
- MYS — MYSTICAL TALENT: 6 = [INT + MAF + PHL] / 5

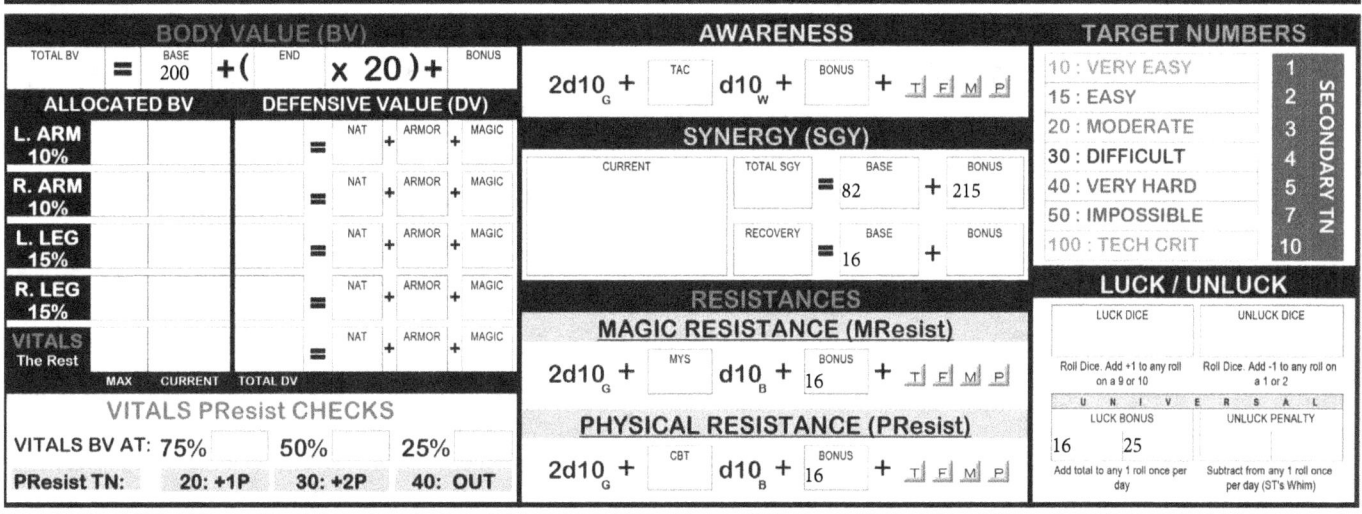

BODY VALUE (BV)

| TOTAL BV | = | BASE 200 | +(| END x 20)+ | BONUS |

ALLOCATED BV · DEFENSIVE VALUE (DV)

		NAT + ARMOR + MAGIC
L. ARM 10%	=	
R. ARM 10%	=	
L. LEG 15%	=	
R. LEG 15%	=	
VITALS The Rest	=	
	MAX · CURRENT · TOTAL DV	

VITALS PResist CHECKS

VITALS BV AT: 75% · 50% · 25%

PResist TN: 20: +1P · 30: +2P · 40: OUT

AWARENESS

$2d10_G +$ TAC $d10_W +$ BONUS $+$ T F M P

SYNERGY (SGY)

| CURRENT | TOTAL SGY = 82 | + | BASE 215 | BONUS |
| | RECOVERY = 16 | + | BASE | BONUS |

RESISTANCES

MAGIC RESISTANCE (MResist)

$2d10_G +$ MYS $d10_B +$ BONUS 16 $+$ T F M P

PHYSICAL RESISTANCE (PResist)

$2d10_G +$ CBT $d10_B +$ BONUS 16 $+$ T F M P

TARGET NUMBERS

10 : VERY EASY	1
15 : EASY	2
20 : MODERATE	3
30 : DIFFICULT	4
40 : VERY HARD	5
50 : IMPOSSIBLE	7
100 : TECH CRIT	10

(SECONDARY TN)

LUCK / UNLUCK

LUCK DICE	UNLUCK DICE
Roll Dice. Add +1 to any roll on a 9 or 10	Roll Dice. Add -1 to any roll on a 1 or 2

UNIVERSAL

LUCK BONUS	UNLUCK PENALTY
16 · 25	
Add total to any 1 roll once per day	Subtract from any 1 roll once per day (ST's Whim)

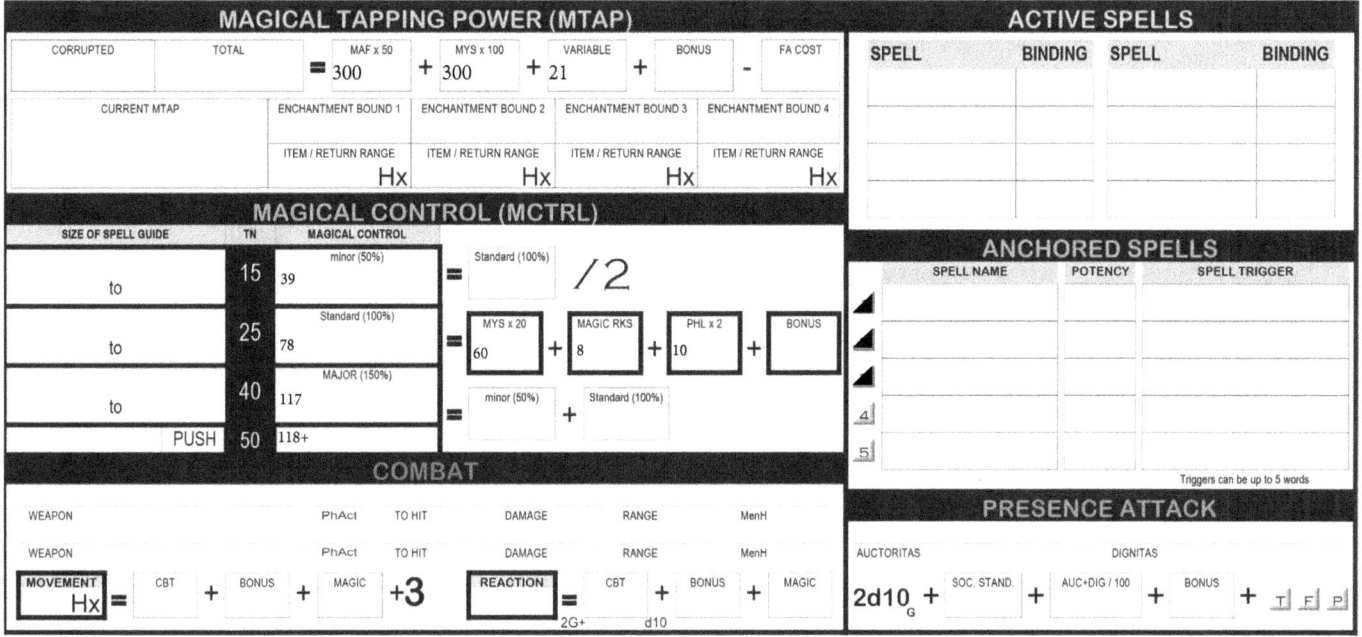

MAGICAL TAPPING POWER (MTAP)

| CORRUPTED | TOTAL | = | MAF x 50 300 | + | MYS x 100 300 | + | VARIABLE 21 | + | BONUS | - | FA COST |

| CURRENT MTAP | ENCHANTMENT BOUND 1 | ENCHANTMENT BOUND 2 | ENCHANTMENT BOUND 3 | ENCHANTMENT BOUND 4 |
| | ITEM / RETURN RANGE Hx | ITEM / RETURN RANGE Hx | ITEM / RETURN RANGE Hx | ITEM / RETURN RANGE Hx |

MAGICAL CONTROL (MCTRL)

SIZE OF SPELL GUIDE	TN	MAGICAL CONTROL
to	15	minor (50%) 39
to	25	Standard (100%) 78
to	40	MAJOR (150%) 117
PUSH	50	118+

Standard (100%) = /2

MYS x 20 60 + MAGIC RKS 8 + PHL x 2 10 + BONUS

minor (50%) + Standard (100%)

ACTIVE SPELLS

SPELL	BINDING	SPELL	BINDING

ANCHORED SPELLS

SPELL NAME	POTENCY	SPELL TRIGGER
4		
5		

Triggers can be up to 5 words

COMBAT

| WEAPON | PhAct | TO HIT | DAMAGE | RANGE | MenH |
| WEAPON | PhAct | TO HIT | DAMAGE | RANGE | MenH |

MOVEMENT Hx = CBT + BONUS + MAGIC +3

REACTION = CBT + BONUS + MAGIC
2G+ · d10

PRESENCE ATTACK

AUCTORITAS	DIGNITAS

$2d10_G +$ SOC. STAND. $+$ AUC+DIG / 100 $+$ BONUS $+$ T F P

IMMORTAL EMPIRES™

SKILLS 1

200 Skill Points to spend Anywhere! Remember, each Rank costs its own number in Skill Points, and each Rank must be bought sequentially!

ACADEMIC/SCHOLARLY SKILLS

COST MODIFIER	
CATEGORY BONUS	
	TAC

GENERAL

Ranks	Mods	Skill
1 2 3 4 5	T F M P	Administration
1 2 3 4 5	T F M P	Business
1 2 3 4 5	T F M P	Appraising
1 2 3 4 5	T F M P	Cartography
1 2 3 4 5	T F M P	Engineering
1 2 3 4 5	T F M P	Geography
1 2 3 4 5	T F M P	History
1 2 3 4 5	T F M P	Law
1 2 3 4 5	T F M P	Numbers
1 2 3 4 5	T F M P	Scribing
1 2 3 4 5	T F M P	Teaching
1 2 3 4 5	T F M P	Trade Lore

LANGUAGES

Ranks	Mods	Skill
1 2 3 4 5	T F M P	Ancient Races
1 2 3 4 5	T F M P	Fey Races
1 2 3 4 5	T F M P	Modern Races

MEDICINE

Ranks	Mods	Skill
1 2 3 4 5	T F M P	Chirurgy
1 2 3 4 5	T F M P	First Aid
1 2 3 4 5	T F M P	Gen. Medicine
1 2 3 4 5	T F M P	Veterinary

SCIENCE

Ranks	Mods	Skill
1 2 3 4 5	T F M P	Astronomy
1 2 3 4 5	T F M P	Biology
1 2 3 4 5	T F M P	Forensics
1 2 3 4 5	T F M P	Metallurgy
1 2 3 4 5	T F M P	Metaphysics
1 2 3 4 5	T F M P	Natural Earth

COMBAT/MILITARY SKILLS

COST MODIFIER	
CATEGORY BONUS	
	CBT

GENERAL

Ranks	Mods	Skill
1 2 3 4 5	T F M P	Footwork
1 2 3 4 5	T F M P	Special Moves
1 2 3 4 5	T F M P	Surprise

MINOR FIGHTING ARTS

Ranks	Mods	Skill
1 2 3 4 5	T F M P	Capua
1 2 3 4 5	T F M P	E. S. Wrestling
1 2 3 4 5	T F M P	Gladiator

TACTICS

Ranks	Mods	Skill
1 2 3 4 5	T F M P	Air
1 2 3 4 5	T F M P	Criminal
1 2 3 4 5	T F M P	Land
1 2 3 4 5	T F M P	Magical
1 2 3 4 5	T F M P	Naval

WEAPONRY

Ranks	Mods	Skill
1 2 3 4 5	T F M P	Commoner
1 2 3 4 5	T F M P	Bows
1 2 3 4 5	T F M P	Cleaving
1 2 3 4 5	T F M P	Crossbows
1 2 3 4 5	T F M P	Crushing
1 2 3 4 5	T F M P	Dodge
1 2 3 4 5	T F M P	Exotic
1 2 3 4 5	T F M P	Long Blades
1 2 3 4 5	T F M P	Martial
1 2 3 4 5	T F M P	Polearms
1 2 3 4 5	T F M P	Shields
1 2 3 4 5	T F M P	Short Blades
1 2 3 4 5	T F M P	Siege Engines
1 2 3 4 5	T F M P	Unarmed

MAGICAL/MYSTICAL SKILLS

COST MODIFIER	
CATEGORY BONUS	
	MYS

GENERAL

Ranks	Mods	Skill
1 2 3 4 5	T F M P	Calligraphy
1 2 3 4 5	T F M P	Herbalism
1 2 3 4 5	T F M P	Levlines
1 2 3 4 5	T F M P	Magical Theory
1 2 3 4 5	T F M P	Philosophy

LORE

Ranks	Mods	Skill
1 2 3 4 5	T F M P	Arcane
1 2 3 4 5	T F M P	Dimensions
1 2 3 4 5	T F M P	Dragon
1 2 3 4 5	T F M P	Faerie
1 2 3 4 5	T F M P	Machine
1 2 3 4 5	T F M P	Undead

MAGICAL

Ranks	Mods	Skill
1 2 3 4 5	T F M P	Candle Magic
1 2 3 4 5	T F M P	Casting
1 2 3 4 5	T F M P	Centering
1 2 3 4 5	T F M P	Constructs
1 2 3 4 5	T F M P	Weave Celerity

MYSTICAL

Ranks	Mods	Skill
1 2 3 4 5	T F M P	Apothecary
1 2 3 4 5	T F M P	Aura Reading
1 2 3 4 5	T F M P	Counterspell
1 2 3 4 5	T F M P	Hypnotism
1 2 3 4 5	T F M P	Illusion
1 2 3 4 5	T F M P	Pyrotechnics
1 2 3 4 5	T F M P	Ritual Structures
1 2 3 4 5	T F M P	Secret Rites
1 2 3 4 5	T F M P	Soothsaying

Ancient Languages / Modern Languages

Ancient Languages	Modern Languages
1)	1)
2)	2)
3)	3)
4)	4)
5)	5)

Fey Languages / Law

Fey Languages	Law
1)	1)
2)	2)
3)	3)
4)	4)
5)	5)

Geography / Engineering

Geography	Engineering
1)	1)
2)	2)
3)	3)
4)	4)
5)	5)

Magical Access Chart

TRADITION:	Coven				
ALTERATION	✓ m S M	- m S M	- m S M	- m S M	- m S M
BENEDICTION	(orange)	- m S M	- m S M	- m S M	- m S M
CHARM	(orange)	- m S M	- m S M	- m S M	- m S M
CONJURING	- m S ✓	- m S M	- m S M	- m S M	- m S M
CURATIVE	(orange)	- m S M	- m S M	- m S M	- m S M
DEFENSIVE	- m S ✓	- m S M	- m S M	- m S M	- m S M
DIVINATION	(orange)	- m S M	- m S M	- m S M	- m S M
ENCHANTING	(orange)	- m S M	- m S M	- m S M	- m S M
GLIMMERING	- m ✓ M	- m S M	- m S M	- m S M	- m S M
OFFENSIVE	- m ✓ M	- m S M	- m S M	- m S M	- m S M
SHAPESHIFTING	- ✓ S M	- m S M	- m S M	- m S M	- m S M
TIME	✓ m S M	- m S M	- m S M	- m S M	- m S M
TRAVEL	- m ✓ M	- m S M	- m S M	- m S M	- m S M
UTILITY	- ✓ S M	- m S M	- m S M	- m S M	- m S M
WEATHER	- m S ✓	- m S M	- m S M	- m S M	- m S M

*Achernar can conjure ONLY Air Elementals

IMMORTAL EMPIRES™

SKILLS 2

ARTISTIC/ARTISAN SKILLS

COST MODIFIER	
CATEGORY BONUS	
	ART

GENERAL
1 2 3 4 5 T F M P Cooking
1 2 3 4 5 T F M P Disable Apparatus
1 2 3 4 5 T F M P Disguise
1 2 3 4 5 T F M P Hand Talk
1 2 3 4 5 T F M P Lip Reading

ARTISTIC
1 2 3 4 5 T F M P Acting
1 2 3 4 5 T F M P Dancing
1 2 3 4 5 T F M P Forgery
1 2 3 4 5 T F M P Juggling
1 2 3 4 5 T F M P Lockpicking
1 2 3 4 5 T F M P Musical Comp.
1 2 3 4 5 T F M P Play Instrument
1 2 3 4 5 T F M P Paint/Draw
1 2 3 4 5 T F M P Poetry
1 2 3 4 5 T F M P Singing
1 2 3 4 5 T F M P Sleight of Hand
1 2 3 4 5 T F M P Voice Mimicry

TRADESKILL
1 2 3 4 5 T F M P
1 2 3 4 5 T F M P

SCHOLARLY ARTS
1 2 3 4 5 T F M P Bookbinding
1 2 3 4 5 T F M P Candlemaking
1 2 3 4 5 T F M P Glassblowing
1 2 3 4 5 T F M P Lapidary
1 2 3 4 5 T F M P Mus. Inst. Craft
1 2 3 4 5 T F M P Sculpting

OUTDOOR/ATHLETIC SKILLS

COST MODIFIER	
CATEGORY BONUS	
	END

GENERAL
1 2 3 4 5 T F M P Escape Bonds
1 2 3 4 5 T F M P Evasion
1 2 3 4 5 T F M P Rope Use
1 2 3 4 5 T F M P Stealth
1 2 3 4 5 T F M P Tracking

ANIMAL
1 2 3 4 5 T F M P Animal Handling
1 2 3 4 5 T F M P Animal Training
1 2 3 4 5 T F M P Riding, Aerial
1 2 3 4 5 T F M P Riding, Land
1 2 3 4 5 T F M P Riding, Sea Life
1 2 3 4 5 T F M P Zoology

ATHLETIC
1 2 3 4 5 T F M P Acrobatics
1 2 3 4 5 T F M P Charioteering
1 2 3 4 5 T F M P Climbing
1 2 3 4 5 T F M P Spelunking
1 2 3 4 5 T F M P Swimming

OUTDOOR
1 2 3 4 5 T F M P Camouflage
1 2 3 4 5 T F M P Trapping
1 2 3 4 5 T F M P Hunting
1 2 3 4 5 T F M P Horticulture
1 2 3 4 5 T F M P Meteorology
1 2 3 4 5 T F M P Navigation
1 2 3 4 5 T F M P Sailing, Lg. Craft
1 2 3 4 5 T F M P Sailing, Sm. Craft
1 2 3 4 5 T F M P Survival

SOCIAL/POLITICAL SKILLS

COST MODIFIER	
CATEGORY BONUS	
	SOC

GENERAL
1 2 3 4 5 T F M P Acquisition
1 2 3 4 5 T F M P Acumen
1 2 3 4 5 T F M P Games/Gambling
1 2 3 4 5 T F M P Interrogation
1 2 3 4 5 T F M P Intimidation
1 2 3 4 5 T F M P Lying
1 2 3 4 5 T F M P Savvy, Local
1 2 3 4 5 T F M P Savvy, Regional

POLITICAL
1 2 3 4 5 T F M P Bartering
1 2 3 4 5 T F M P Diplomacy
1 2 3 4 5 T F M P Oratory / Debate
1 2 3 4 5 T F M P Politics

SOCIAL
1 2 3 4 5 T F M P Crowdworking
1 2 3 4 5 T F M P Info. Gathering
1 2 3 4 5 T F M P Leadership
1 2 3 4 5 T F M P Mingling
1 2 3 4 5 T F M P Seduction

SOCIAL CIRCLES
1 2 3 4 5 T F M P Family
1 2 3 4 5 T F M P Social Classes
1 2 3 4 5 T F M P
1 2 3 4 5 T F M P
1 2 3 4 5 T F M P
1 2 3 4 5 T F M P

FAVOR BANK

TYPE	FAVORS	REQUESTS
SMALL		
BIG		
HUGE		
GUBERNATORIAL		
SENETORIAL		
ROYAL		
IMPERIAL		

EYES AND EARS

YOUR CLIENTS

NAME	BUSINESS	IMPORTANCE
PLOT	LOYALTY	WHERE	CLIENT PIN?

NAME	BUSINESS	IMPORTANCE
PLOT	LOYALTY	WHERE	CLIENT PIN?

NAME	BUSINESS	IMPORTANCE
PLOT	LOYALTY	WHERE	CLIENT PIN?

ENEMIES' CLIENTS

NAME	BUSINESS	IMPORTANCE
PLOT	LOYALTY	WHERE	CLIENT PIN?

NAME	BUSINESS	IMPORTANCE
PLOT	LOYALTY	WHERE	CLIENT PIN?

NAME	BUSINESS	IMPORTANCE
PLOT	LOYALTY	WHERE	CLIENT PIN?

PLOTS
A
B
C
D
E
F
G
H
I
J
K

ESTATES

NAME	LOCATION	VALUE	REVENUE
SOLDIERS	Gr. Champions	Champions	Elite	Above Average	Average	Below Average	Non-Military Population

NAME	LOCATION	VALUE	REVENUE
SOLDIERS	Gr. Champions	Champions	Elite	Above Average	Average	Below Average	Non-Military Population

MISCELLANEOUS

EQUIPMENT

PACK 1

ITEM	QTY.

PACK 2

ITEM	QTY.

PACK 3

ITEM	QTY.

PACK 4

ITEM	QTY.

Tiny items such as vials stack up to 10 in the same slot, but mixing different small items in the same slot is not allowed. Thank you. --The Presidium

MONEY

CARRIED

GOLD	
SILVER	
COPPER	

1 GOLD = 25 SILVER = 100 COPPER

SPELL BATTERIES

POWER BASES

Power Base	Rating
Criminal	
Foreign	
Magical	
Military	
Political	
Popular	

ITEMS EQUIPPED

LOCATION	ITEM	DESCRIPTION
HEAD		
NECK		
TORSO		
ARMOR		
ARMS		
HANDS		
WAIST		
RING 1		
RING 2		
LEGS		
FEET		
BACK		
SHIELD		

COMPANIONS / BONDED ANIMALS

NAME			
PHQ	RACE		P Attk
PHL	HGT		DMG
AGL	WGT		M Attk
COR	VOC		POT
INT	RANK		PResist
INS	AWARE		MResist
WIL	MVT		BV
EMP	DODGE		DV
MAF	SGY		MTAP
NAME			
PHQ	RACE		P Attk
PHL	HGT		DMG
AGL	WGT		M Attk
COR	VOC		POT
INT	RANK		PResist
INS	AWARE		MResist
WIL	MVT		BV
EMP	DODGE		DV
MAF	SGY		MTAP

TRAITS / FLAWS

PHYSICAL	+5 Spell Battery, +3 Contortionist, +1 Agile
LEARNING	+5 Favored by Antara, +3 Wonder Worker, +1 SK:Casting
SOCIAL	+5 Get out of Jail Free Card, +3 Well-known, +1 Fence

MEMORIZED

FIGHTING ART POWERS

Physical	
Intellectual	
Spiritual	
Arcane	

HIRELINGS

SKILL PACKAGES

PACKAGE	RATIO
Coven Member	50 : 1
	: 1
	: 1
	: 1
	: 1
TOTAL	: 1

YOU select Achernar's Talents (Synergy), as a R8 Guardian (AR59 to see what he gets).

IMMORTAL EMPIRES™
CHARACTER RECORD

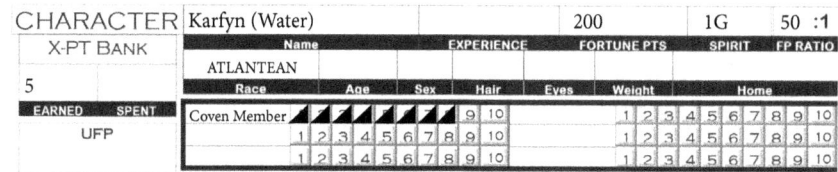

CHARACTER	Karfyn (Water)		200	1G	50 :1

X-PT BANK	Name	EXPERIENCE	FORTUNE PTS	SPIRIT	FP RATIO
5	ATLANTEAN				
EARNED SPENT	Race	Age	Sex	Hair	Eyes	Weight	Home
UFP	Coven Member	9 10				1 2 3 4 5 6 7 8 9 10

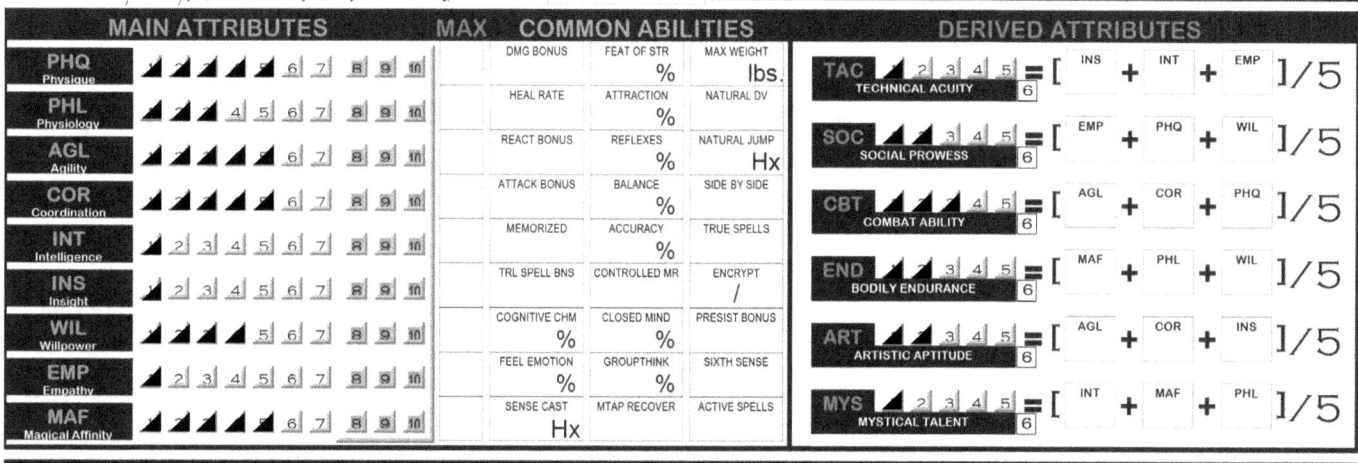

MAIN ATTRIBUTES

- PHQ Physique — 6 7 8 9 10
- PHL Physiology — 4 5 6 7 8 9 10
- AGL Agility — 6 7 8 9 10
- COR Coordination — 6 7 8 9 10
- INT Intelligence — 2 3 4 5 6 7 8 9 10
- INS Insight — 2 3 4 5 6 7 8 9 10
- WIL Willpower — 5 6 7 8 9 10
- EMP Empathy — 2 3 4 5 6 7 8 9 10
- MAF Magical Affinity — 6 7 8 9 10

MAX COMMON ABILITIES

DMG BONUS	FEAT OF STR	MAX WEIGHT lbs.
HEAL RATE	ATTRACTION %	NATURAL DV
REACT BONUS	REFLEXES %	NATURAL JUMP Hx
ATTACK BONUS	BALANCE %	SIDE BY SIDE
MEMORIZED	ACCURACY %	TRUE SPELLS
TRL SPELL BNS	CONTROLLED MR	ENCRYPT /
COGNITIVE CHM %	CLOSED MIND %	PRESIST BONUS
FEEL EMOTION %	GROUPTHINK %	SIXTH SENSE
SENSE CAST Hx	MTAP RECOVER	ACTIVE SPELLS

DERIVED ATTRIBUTES

- TAC TECHNICAL ACUITY = [INS + INT + EMP]/5   6
- SOC SOCIAL PROWESS = [EMP + PHQ + WIL]/5   6
- CBT COMBAT ABILITY = [AGL + COR + PHQ]/5   6
- END BODILY ENDURANCE = [MAF + PHL + WIL]/5   6
- ART ARTISTIC APTITUDE = [AGL + COR + INS]/5   6
- MYS MYSTICAL TALENT = [INT + MAF + PHL]/5   6

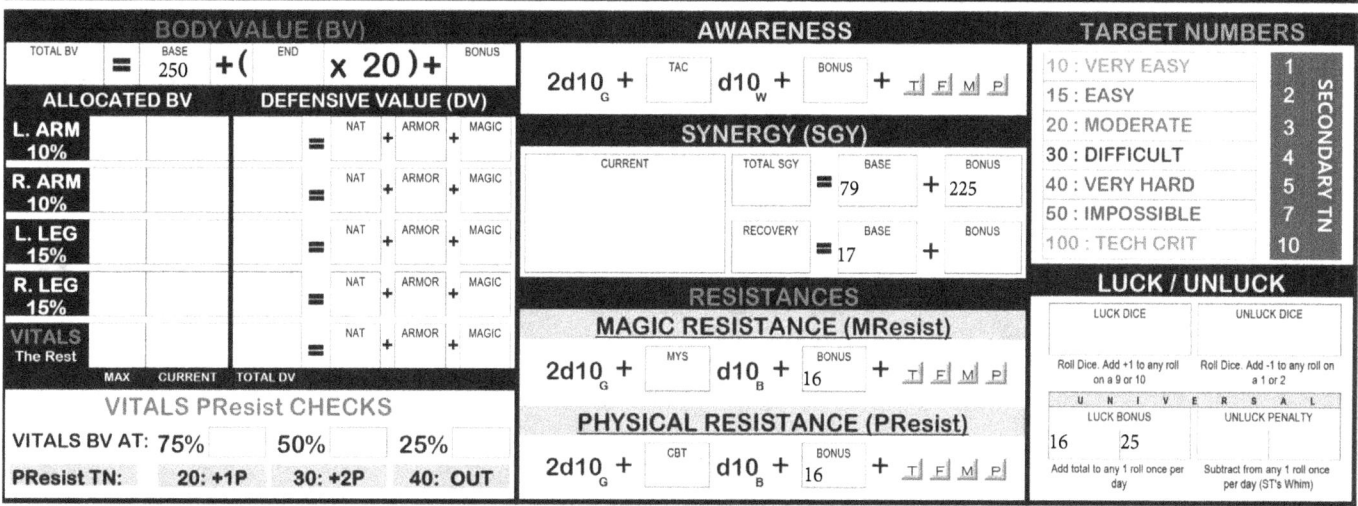

BODY VALUE (BV)

| TOTAL BV | = | BASE 250 | +(END x 20)+ | BONUS |

ALLOCATED BV / DEFENSIVE VALUE (DV)

L. ARM 10%	=	NAT + ARMOR + MAGIC
R. ARM 10%	=	NAT + ARMOR + MAGIC
L. LEG 15%	=	NAT + ARMOR + MAGIC
R. LEG 15%	=	NAT + ARMOR + MAGIC
VITALS The Rest	=	NAT + ARMOR + MAGIC

MAX CURRENT TOTAL DV

VITALS PResist CHECKS

VITALS BV AT: 75%   50%   25%
PResist TN: 20: +1P   30: +2P   40: OUT

AWARENESS

$2d10_G$ + [TAC] $d10_w$ + [BONUS] + T F M P

SYNERGY (SGY)

| CURRENT | TOTAL SGY = 79 | + | BONUS 225 |
| | RECOVERY = 17 | + | BASE | BONUS |

RESISTANCES

MAGIC RESISTANCE (MResist)

$2d10_G$ + [MYS] $d10_B$ + [BONUS 16] + T F M P

PHYSICAL RESISTANCE (PResist)

$2d10_G$ + [CBT] $d10_B$ + [BONUS 16] + T F M P

TARGET NUMBERS

10 : VERY EASY	1
15 : EASY	2
20 : MODERATE	3
30 : DIFFICULT	4 / 5
40 : VERY HARD	6
50 : IMPOSSIBLE	7
100 : TECH CRIT	10

SECONDARY TN

LUCK / UNLUCK

| LUCK DICE | UNLUCK DICE |
| Roll Dice. Add +1 to any roll on a 9 or 10 | Roll Dice. Add -1 to any roll on a 1 or 2 |

UNIVERSAL

LUCK BONUS	UNLUCK PENALTY
16 25	
Add total to any 1 roll once per day	Subtract from any 1 roll once per day (ST's Whim)

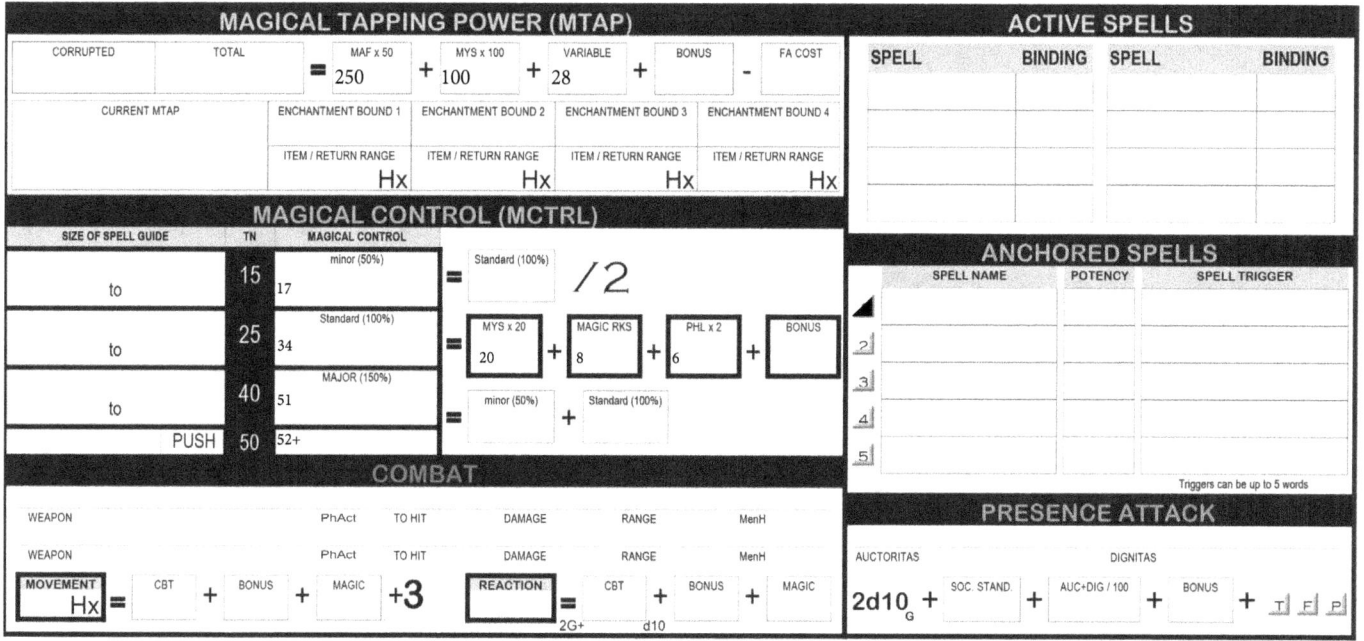

MAGICAL TAPPING POWER (MTAP)

| CORRUPTED | TOTAL | = MAF x 50 250 | + MYS x 100 100 | + VARIABLE 28 | + BONUS | - FA COST |

| CURRENT MTAP | ENCHANTMENT BOUND 1 | ENCHANTMENT BOUND 2 | ENCHANTMENT BOUND 3 | ENCHANTMENT BOUND 4 |
| | ITEM / RETURN RANGE Hx | ITEM / RETURN RANGE Hx | ITEM / RETURN RANGE Hx | ITEM / RETURN RANGE Hx |

MAGICAL CONTROL (MCTRL)

SIZE OF SPELL GUIDE	TN	MAGICAL CONTROL
to	15	minor (50%) 17
to	25	Standard (100%) 34
to	40	MAJOR (150%) 51
PUSH	50	52+

Standard (100%) /2

= MYS x 20 20 + MAGIC RKS 8 + PHL x 2 6 + BONUS

= minor (50%) + Standard (100%)

ACTIVE SPELLS

SPELL	BINDING	SPELL	BINDING

ANCHORED SPELLS

SPELL NAME	POTENCY	SPELL TRIGGER
1		
2		
3		
4		
5		

Triggers can be up to 5 words

COMBAT

| WEAPON | | PhAct | TO HIT | DAMAGE | RANGE | MenH |
| WEAPON | | PhAct | TO HIT | DAMAGE | RANGE | MenH |

MOVEMENT Hx = CBT + BONUS + MAGIC +3

REACTION = CBT + BONUS + MAGIC 2G+ d10

PRESENCE ATTACK

| AUCTORITAS | DIGNITAS |

$2d10_G$ + [SOC. STAND.] + [AUC+DIG / 100] + [BONUS] + T F P

SKILLS 1

CHARACTER	Karfyn (Water)

200 Skill Points to spend Anywhere! Remember, each Rank costs its own number in Skill Points, and each Rank must be bought sequentially!

ACADEMIC/SCHOLARLY SKILLS

COST MODIFIER	
CATEGORY BONUS	
	TAC

GENERAL
1 2 3 4 5 T F M P Administration
1 2 3 4 5 T F M P Business
1 2 3 4 5 T F M P Appraising
1 2 3 4 5 T F M P Cartography
1 2 3 4 5 T F M P Engineering
1 2 3 4 5 T F M P Geography
1 2 3 4 5 T F M P History
1 2 3 4 5 T F M P Law
1 2 3 4 5 T F M P Numbers
1 2 3 4 5 T F M P Scribing
1 2 3 4 5 T F M P Teaching
1 2 3 4 5 T F M P Trade Lore

LANGUAGES
1 2 3 4 5 T F M P Ancient Races
1 2 3 4 5 T F M P Fey Races
1 2 3 4 5 T F M P Modern Races

MEDICINE
1 2 3 4 5 T F M P Chirurgy
1 2 3 4 5 T F M P First Aid
1 2 3 4 5 T F M P Gen. Medicine
1 2 3 4 5 T F M P Veterinary

SCIENCE
1 2 3 4 5 T F M P Astronomy
1 2 3 4 5 T F M P Biology
1 2 3 4 5 T F M P Forensics
1 2 3 4 5 T F M P Metallurgy
1 2 3 4 5 T F M P Metaphysics
1 2 3 4 5 T F M P Natural Earth

COMBAT/MILITARY SKILLS

COST MODIFIER	
CATEGORY BONUS	
	CBT

GENERAL
1 2 3 4 5 T F M P Footwork
1 2 3 4 5 T F M P Special Moves
1 2 3 4 5 T F M P Surprise

MINOR FIGHTING ARTS
1 2 3 4 5 T F M P Capua
1 2 3 4 5 T F M P E. S. Wrestling
1 2 3 4 5 T F M P Gladiator

TACTICS
1 2 3 4 5 T F M P Air
1 2 3 4 5 T F M P Criminal
1 2 3 4 5 T F M P Land
1 2 3 4 5 T F M P Magical
1 2 3 4 5 T F M P Naval

WEAPONRY
1 2 3 4 5 T F M P Commoner
1 2 3 4 5 T F M P Bows
1 2 3 4 5 T F M P Cleaving
1 2 3 4 5 T F M P Crossbows
1 2 3 4 5 T F M P Crushing
1 2 3 4 5 T F M P Dodge
1 2 3 4 5 T F M P Exotic
1 2 3 4 5 T F M P Long Blades
1 2 3 4 5 T F M P Martial
1 2 3 4 5 T F M P Polearms
1 2 3 4 5 T F M P Shields
1 2 3 4 5 T F M P Short Blades
1 2 3 4 5 T F M P Siege Engines
1 2 3 4 5 T F M P Unarmed

MAGICAL/MYSTICAL SKILLS

COST MODIFIER	
CATEGORY BONUS	
	MYS

GENERAL
1 2 3 4 5 T F M P Calligraphy
1 2 3 4 5 T F M P Herbalism
1 2 3 4 5 T F M P Leylines
1 2 3 4 5 T F M P Magical Theory
1 2 3 4 5 T F M P Philosophy

LORE
1 2 3 4 5 T F M P Arcane
1 2 3 4 5 T F M P Dimensions
1 2 3 4 5 T F M P Dragon
1 2 3 4 5 T F M P Faerie
1 2 3 4 5 T F M P Machine
1 2 3 4 5 T F M P Undead

MAGICAL
1 2 3 4 5 T F M P Candle Magic
1 2 3 4 5 T F M P Casting
1 2 3 4 5 T F M P Centering
1 2 3 4 5 T F M P Constructs
1 2 3 4 5 T F M P Weave Celerity

MYSTICAL
1 2 3 4 5 T F M P Apothecary
1 2 3 4 5 T F M P Aura Reading
1 2 3 4 5 T F M P Counterspell
1 2 3 4 5 T F M P Hypnotism
1 2 3 4 5 T F M P Illusion
1 2 3 4 5 T F M P Pyrotechnics
1 2 3 4 5 T F M P Ritual Structures
1 2 3 4 5 T F M P Secret Rites
1 2 3 4 5 T F M P Soothsaying

Ancient Languages
1)
2)
3)
4)
5)

Modern Languages
1)
2)
3)
4)
5)

Fey Languages
1)
2)
3)
4)
5)

Law
1)
2)
3)
4)
5)

Geography
1)
2)
3)
4)
5)

Engineering
1)
2)
3)
4)
5)

Magical Access Chart

TRADITION:	Coven				
ALTERATION	- m S M✓	- m S M	- m S M	- m S M	- m S M
BENEDICTION	▓▓▓	- m S M	- m S M	- m S M	- m S M
CHARM	▓▓▓	- m S M	- m S M	- m S M	- m S M
CONJURING	- m S M✓	- m S M	- m S M	- m S M	- m S M
CURATIVE	▓▓▓	- m S M	- m S M	- m S M	- m S M
DEFENSIVE	- m✓ S M	- m S M	- m S M	- m S M	- m S M
DIVINATION	- m S M✓	- m S M	- m S M	- m S M	- m S M
ENCHANTING	▓▓▓	- m S M	- m S M	- m S M	- m S M
GLIMMERING	- m S✓ M	- m S M	- m S M	- m S M	- m S M
OFFENSIVE	- m✓ S M	- m S M	- m S M	- m S M	- m S M
SHAPESHIFTING	- m S✓ M	- m S M	- m S M	- m S M	- m S M
TIME	✓ m S M	- m S M	- m S M	- m S M	- m S M
TRAVEL	✓ m S M	- m S M	- m S M	- m S M	- m S M
UTILITY	- m S M	- m S M	- m S M	- m S M	- m S M
WEATHER	▓▓▓	- m S M	- m S M	- m S M	- m S M

*Karfyn can conjure ONLY Water Elementals

SKILLS 2

ARTISTIC/ARTISAN SKILLS

COST MODIFIER	
CATEGORY BONUS	ART

GENERAL
- 1 2 3 4 5 T F M P — Cooking
- 1 2 3 4 5 T F M P — Disable Apparatus
- 1 2 3 4 5 T F M P — Disguise
- 1 2 3 4 5 T F M P — Hand Talk
- 1 2 3 4 5 T F M P — Lip Reading

ARTISTIC
- 1 2 3 4 5 T F M P — Acting
- 1 2 3 4 5 T F M P — Dancing
- 1 2 3 4 5 T F M P — Forgery
- 1 2 3 4 5 T F M P — Juggling
- 1 2 3 4 5 T F M P — Lockpicking
- 1 2 3 4 5 T F M P — Musical Comp.
- 1 2 3 4 5 T F M P — Play Instrument
- 1 2 3 4 5 T F M P — Paint/Draw
- 1 2 3 4 5 T F M P — Poetry
- 1 2 3 4 5 T F M P — Singing
- 1 2 3 4 5 T F M P — Sleight of Hand
- 1 2 3 4 5 T F M P — Voice Mimicry

TRADESKILL
- 1 2 3 4 5 T F M P —
- 1 2 3 4 5 T F M P —

SCHOLARLY ARTS
- 1 2 3 4 5 T F M P — Bookbinding
- 1 2 3 4 5 T F M P — Candlemaking
- 1 2 3 4 5 T F M P — Glassblowing
- 1 2 3 4 5 T F M P — Lapidary
- 1 2 3 4 5 T F M P — Mus. Inst. Craft
- 1 2 3 4 5 T F M P — Sculpting

OUTDOOR/ATHLETIC SKILLS

COST MODIFIER	
CATEGORY BONUS	END

GENERAL
- 1 2 3 4 5 T F M P — Escape Bonds
- 1 2 3 4 5 T F M P — Evasion
- 1 2 3 4 5 T F M P — Rope Use
- 1 2 3 4 5 T F M P — Stealth
- 1 2 3 4 5 T F M P — Tracking

ANIMAL
- 1 2 3 4 5 T F M P — Animal Handling
- 1 2 3 4 5 T F M P — Animal Training
- 1 2 3 4 5 T F M P — Riding, Aerial
- 1 2 3 4 5 T F M P — Riding, Land
- 1 2 3 4 5 T F M P — Riding, Sea Life
- 1 2 3 4 5 T F M P — Zoology

ATHLETIC
- 1 2 3 4 5 T F M P — Acrobatics
- 1 2 3 4 5 T F M P — Charioteering
- 1 2 3 4 5 T F M P — Climbing
- 1 2 3 4 5 T F M P — Spelunking
- 1 2 3 4 5 T F M P — Swimming

OUTDOOR
- 1 2 3 4 5 T F M P — Camouflage
- 1 2 3 4 5 T F M P — Trapping
- 1 2 3 4 5 T F M P — Hunting
- 1 2 3 4 5 T F M P — Horticulture
- 1 2 3 4 5 T F M P — Meteorology
- 1 2 3 4 5 T F M P — Navigation
- 1 2 3 4 5 T F M P — Sailing, Lg. Craft
- 1 2 3 4 5 T F M P — Sailing, Sm. Craft
- 1 2 3 4 5 T F M P — Survival

SOCIAL/POLITICAL SKILLS

COST MODIFIER	
CATEGORY BONUS	SOC

GENERAL
- 1 2 3 4 5 T F M P — Acquisition
- 1 2 3 4 5 T F M P — Acumen
- 1 2 3 4 5 T F M P — Games/Gambling
- 1 2 3 4 5 T F M P — Interrogation
- 1 2 3 4 5 T F M P — Intimidation
- 1 2 3 4 5 T F M P — Lying
- 1 2 3 4 5 T F M P — Savvy, Local
- 1 2 3 4 5 T F M P — Savvy, Regional

POLITICAL
- 1 2 3 4 5 T F M P — Bartering
- 1 2 3 4 5 T F M P — Diplomacy
- 1 2 3 4 5 T F M P — Oratory / Debate
- 1 2 3 4 5 T F M P — Politics

SOCIAL
- 1 2 3 4 5 T F M P — Crowdworking
- 1 2 3 4 5 T F M P — Info. Gathering
- 1 2 3 4 5 T F M P — Leadership
- 1 2 3 4 5 T F M P — Mingling
- 1 2 3 4 5 T F M P — Seduction

SOCIAL CIRCLES
- 1 2 3 4 5 T F M P — Family
- 1 2 3 4 5 T F M P — Social Classes
- 1 2 3 4 5 T F M P —
- 1 2 3 4 5 T F M P —
- 1 2 3 4 5 T F M P —

FAVOR BANK

TYPE	FAVORS	REQUESTS
SMALL		
BIG		
HUGE		
GUBERNATORIAL		
SENETORIAL		
ROYAL		
IMPERIAL		

EYES AND EARS

YOUR CLIENTS

NAME	BUSINESS	IMPORTANCE
PLOT	LOYALTY	WHERE	CLIENT PIN?

NAME	BUSINESS	IMPORTANCE
PLOT	LOYALTY	WHERE	CLIENT PIN?

NAME	BUSINESS	IMPORTANCE
PLOT	LOYALTY	WHERE	CLIENT PIN?

ENEMIES' CLIENTS

NAME	BUSINESS	IMPORTANCE
PLOT	LOYALTY	WHERE	CLIENT PIN?

NAME	BUSINESS	IMPORTANCE
PLOT	LOYALTY	WHERE	CLIENT PIN?

NAME	BUSINESS	IMPORTANCE
PLOT	LOYALTY	WHERE	CLIENT PIN?

PLOTS
A
B
C
D
E
F
G
H
I
J
K

ESTATES

NAME	LOCATION	VALUE	REVENUE
SOLDIERS	Gr. Champions	Champions	Elite	Above Average	Average	Below Average	Non-Military Population

NAME	LOCATION	VALUE	REVENUE
SOLDIERS	Gr. Champions	Champions	Elite	Above Average	Average	Below Average	Non-Military Population

MISCELLANEOUS

EQUIPMENT

PACK 1

ITEM	QTY.

PACK 2

ITEM	QTY.

PACK 3

ITEM	QTY.

PACK 4

ITEM	QTY.

Tiny Items such as vials stack up to 10 in the same slot, but mixing different small items in the same slot is not allowed. Thank you. --The Presidium

MONEY

CARRIED

GOLD	
SILVER	
COPPER	

1 GOLD = 25 SILVER = 100 COPPER

SPELL BATTERIES

POWER BASES

Power Base	Rating
Criminal	
Foreign	
Magical	
Military	
Political	
Popular	

ITEMS EQUIPPED

LOCATION	ITEM	DESCRIPTION
HEAD		
NECK		
TORSO		
ARMOR		
ARMS		
HANDS		
WAIST		
RING 1		
RING 2		
LEGS		
FEET		
BACK		
SHIELD		

COMPANIONS / BONDED ANIMALS

NAME			
PHQ	RACE		P Attk
PHL	HGT		DMG
AGL	WGT		M Attk
COR	VOC		POT
INT	RANK		PResist
INS	AWARE		MResist
WIL	MVT		BV
EMP	DODGE		DV
MAF	SGY		MTAP
NAME			
PHQ	RACE		P Attk
PHL	HGT		DMG
AGL	WGT		M Attk
COR	VOC		POT
INT	RANK		PResist
INS	AWARE		MResist
WIL	MVT		BV
EMP	DODGE		DV
MAF	SGY		MTAP

TRAITS / FLAWS

PHYSICAL	+5 Physically Resistant, +3 Cornfed Body Type, +1 Hidden Skin Pouch
LEARNING	+5 Favored by Antara, +3 Celeritous Vision, +1 SK:Surprise
SOCIAL	+5 Social Genius, +3 Influential Buddy, +1 Life of the Party

MEMORIZED

FIGHTING ART POWERS

Physical	
Intellectual	
Spiritual	
Arcane	

HIRELINGS

SKILL PACKAGES

PACKAGE	RATIO
Coven Member	50 : 1
	: 1
	: 1
	: 1
	: 1
TOTAL	: 1

YOU select Karfyn's Talents (Synergy), as a R8 Guardian (AR59 to see what he gets).